Absolute Zero

Helen Cresswell

UNIVERSITY PRESS

OXFORD
UNIVERSITY PRESS

Great Clarendon Street, Oxford OX2 6DP

Oxford University Press is a department of the University of Oxford.
It furthers the University's objective of excellence in research, scholarship,
and education by publishing worldwide in

Oxford   New York

Auckland   Cape Town   Dar es Salaam   Hong Kong   Karachi
Kuala Lumpur   Madrid   Melbourne   Mexico City   Nairobi
New Delhi   Shanghai   Taipei   Toronto

With offices in

Argentina   Austria   Brazil   Chile   Czech Republic   France   Greece
Guatemala   Hungary   Italy   Japan   South Korea   Poland   Portugal
Singapore   Switzerland   Thailand   Turkey   Ukraine   Vietnam

Oxford is a registered trade mark of Oxford University Press
in the UK and in certain other countries

British Library Cataloguing in Publication Data

Data available

ISBN-13: 978-0-19-275400-4
ISBN-10: 0-19-275400-9

1 3 5 7 9 10 8 6 4 2

Typeset by Palimpsest Book Production Limited, Polmont, Stirlingshire

Printed in Great Britain by Cox & Wyman Ltd, Reading, Berkshire

To Candida with love

Chapter 1

The whole thing started when Uncle Parker won a cruise in the Caribbean for two after filling in a leaflet he had idly picked up in the village shop. The minute the news was known in the Bagthorpe household disbelief, annoyance, and downright jealousy began to degenerate into what became, inevitably, an All Out Furore.

The company who had promoted this competition sold Sugar-Coated Puffballs breakfast cereal. Mr Bagthorpe immediately stated that Uncle Parker should refuse the prize on moral grounds. Uncle Parker, he said, had never consumed so much as a single Sugar-Coated Puffball in his entire life, and was thus automatically disqualified from reaping a reward for doing so. Mrs Bagthorpe did not agree. Daisy Parker, she said, ate a lot of Sugar-Coated Puffballs, she ate them every day of her life.

In that case, Mr Bagthorpe said, Daisy should have filled in the competition form. He then turned on his own children.

'Don't *you* lot ever eat Sugar-Coated Puffballs?' he demanded. 'What's the matter with you?'

'I do,' said Jack promptly. 'I really like them.'

'So why didn't *you* go in for this thing?'

'I haven't got a leaflet,' Jack said. 'And even if I had, I wouldn't have bothered. Nobody ever wins those things.'

'On the contrary, somebody *does* win them,' said Mr Bagthorpe in a tight voice. 'We *know* that.'

'Why didn't you tell me there was a competition?' asked William. 'Then I could've won a prize.'

'You don't automatically win by filling in a form, you know,' Tess told him. 'Usually some kind of skill is required. And usually the deciding factor is a slogan.'

'So?' said William.

'I'd be better at slogans than you,' said Tess.

She turned not a hair as she spoke. In the Bagthorpe house everybody boasted. It was not called boasting, it was called 'having a just pride in one's own talents and achievements'—a phrase coined by Mrs Bagthorpe, who was very strong on Positive Thinking. The only ones who did not go in for it were Jack and his mongrel dog, Zero. They just kept quiet and lay low, mostly.

'*I*,' interposed Mr Bagthorpe now, 'would be

better than *anybody* at slogans, I believe. And how that layabout insensitive parasite managed to string so many as half a dozen words together is beyond me.'

'Perhaps Aunt Celia helped him,' said Rosie. 'She can do *The Times* crossword three times as quickly as you can, father. *And* she doesn't use dictionaries and things.'

Honesty, especially of the tactless variety, was also a common trait of the Bagthorpe family.

'Nothing to do with it,' said Mr Bagthorpe. 'Any fool can do crosswords. It's creativity that counts.'

'But Aunt Celia writes poetry,' said Rosie, who could be as incorrigible as anyone if she chose, even though she was only just nine.

'Aunt Celia writes poetry,' repeated Mr Bagthorpe. 'So she does. And does anybody ever understand a single word of it?'

No one answered this.

'I spend my entire life wrestling with words,' went on Mr Bagthorpe. (He wrote scripts for television.) 'I live, breathe, sleep, and eat words.'

(This was not strictly true. One thing Mr Bagthorpe never did was eat his words.)

The news of Uncle Parker's win had been conveyed by telephone, and later in the morning he raced up the drive in his usual gravel-scattering style to rub salt in the wound. Jack and Zero were lying on the lawn, the former reading a comic, the latter gnawing a bone. Uncle Parker came to a furious halt and poked his head out of the window.

'Morning,' he said. 'How've they taken it, then?'

'I think you should have waited a bit longer before coming round,' Jack told him. 'They haven't got over it yet.'

'Green as grass, are they?'

'Greener,' Jack told him.

'Your father's hardest hit, I take it?'

'He's livid,' Jack said. 'He says you can't string half a dozen words together.'

'Didn't have to,' said Uncle Parker cheerfully. 'Only five words in my slogan.'

'What was it?' enquired Jack with interest. It suddenly occurred to him that *he* could string five words together, at a pinch.

Uncle Parker cleared his throat.

'Sounds a bit silly in cold blood,' he said, 'even to me. But here goes: *Get Tough with Sugar Puff.*'

There was a silence.

'Is that all?'

'That's it.'

'Well, I'm bound to say,' said Jack at last, 'that

it doesn't sound much. You're pretty lucky to have won a prize with that. If you don't mind my saying.'

Jack was endowed with the Bagthorpian honesty but was not so ruthless with it as the rest. He tried to temper it a little.

'You are absolutely right,' agreed Uncle Parker. 'I would not have given anyone a bar of chocolate for that slogan. I wouldn't have given them a handful of peanuts. But in their wisdom, Messrs Sugar-Coated Puffballs have decided I deserve a Caribbean holiday for it, and who am I to argue?'

'Father's going to argue,' said Jack. 'Come on, Zero.'

He got up and followed the car to the house, to be sure not to miss anything. Uncle Parker was in the kitchen trying to persuade Mrs Fosdyke to give him a cup of coffee. None of the family was yet in evidence though they soon would be. The way Uncle Parker drove, nobody could be unaware of his arrival.

'When Mrs Bagthorpe comes out of her Problems I shall make coffee,' Mrs Fosdyke was saying firmly. (Mrs Bagthorpe did a monthly Agony Column under the name of Stella Bright, and it took a great deal of her time. It also took a great deal out of her.)

Mr Bagthorpe appeared.

'Morning, Henry,' Uncle Parker greeted him. 'Script coming along, is it?'

'What was that slogan, then?' demanded Mr Bagthorpe, dispensing with the niceties.

'It was a bad slogan,' Uncle Parker told him, 'but the others were evidently worse. The more people ask me to repeat it, the less I enjoy doing so. You tell him, Jack.'

'*Get Tough with Sugar Puff*,' said Jack.

Mr Bagthorpe sat down. He shook his head long and hard.

'It's a reflection on the society we live in, of course,' he said at last.

'Oh, it is,' Uncle Parker agreed. 'I deplore it.'

'Hullo, Uncle Park!' Rosie ran in now. 'You are clever winning that prize. And when you and Aunt Celia are away, can Daisy come and stay with us?'

Rosie was the youngest of the Bagthorpe children, and in the position of having no one to look down on. She looked down on Jack, up to a point, although he was older, but Daisy was only four and three quarters and much more easily impressed.

'If that child comes here,' said Mr Bagthorpe, 'it will be up to you, Russell, to pay extra fire cover on the house, and take out policies on all our lives.'

'Including Zero's,' put in Jack.

Not many months previously Daisy had gone through a Pyromaniac Phase. She had started nine fires in one week, three of them serious. The Bagthorpe dining-room was still only partly restored after Grandma's disastrous Birthday Party when Daisy had hidden under the table with two boxes of crackers and one of fireworks.

'She doesn't go in for fires any more,' said Uncle Parker.

'Oh?' Mr Bagthorpe was not comforted. 'So what does she do now for kicks? Poisons people, perhaps—something like that?'

'She is in a very interesting Phase at the present,' said Uncle Parker. 'She is doing all kinds of things.'

'*Can* she come, father?' begged Rosie. 'I think she's really sweet. I'd look after her.'

'I shouldn't think the question will arise, Rosie,' said Mr Bagthorpe. 'I should hardly think your uncle will have the gall to accept this prize.'

'Why's that?' enquired Uncle Parker, tipping back his chair with the air of careless ease that particularly aggravated Mr Bagthorpe.

'It's a moral issue,' said Mr Bagthorpe. 'You have never eaten a Sugar-Coated Puffball in your life.'

'I have not,' conceded Uncle Parker.

'There you are then!' Mr Bagthorpe had the air of a man clinching an argument.

'I don't get your drift,' said Uncle Parker. 'Nothing in the small print says anything about *eating* the wretched stuff. All one had to do was buy a packet and pick up a leaflet. I did both these things. It will, of course, be glorious for Celia and myself, cruising in the Caribbean. I expect, Henry, you wish you had the chance yourself.'

'I wish no such thing!' snapped Mr Bagthorpe. 'There is nothing I can think of I would hate more. Given the choice between the saltmines and the Caribbean, I'd plump for the former any time.'

'Someone might be running a competition for the saltmines,' suggested Uncle Parker. 'You must keep your eyes open.'

'Luckily,' said Mr Bagthorpe, 'I have work to do in life. Luckily, I have a service to give to my fellow men and do not have to fill in my point-less existence wafting round among palm trees drinking gin and tonic by the bucketful.'

'Hallo, Uncle Parker.' William came in. 'Jolly good work. What was the slogan?'

'Tell him, Jack,' said Uncle Parker wearily.

Jack told him. Even he was beginning to tire

of repeating it, and could see how weak it sounded.

'You're joking,' said William after a slight pause.

'No,' said Mr Bagthorpe, 'he is not, unfortunately, joking. I often wonder whether we should have brought children into a world of such colossal triviality.'

'Well, if you don't mind my saying,' said William, with true Bagthorpian ruthlessness, 'I should think the sales of Sugar-Coated Puffballs will plummet when that gets out. Go into a fatal nosedive, I should think.'

'Sugar-Coated Puffballs will be bankrupt within the month,' affirmed Mr Bagthorpe.

'When're you going?' Jack asked. He was going to miss Uncle Parker. He got on well with him, and could feel equal in his company.

'Next week, we thought,' Uncle Parker replied.

Mr Bagthorpe rose.

'I must get back to work,' he said witheringly, and went.

'I saw that competition, Mr Parker,' said Mrs Fosdyke then. 'And d'you know, I nearly went in myself. Worked a slogan out, and all, I did, and never got round to sending it off.'

'What was the slogan?' asked Rosie.

'Well . . .' Mrs Fosdyke cleared her throat, stood up straight and twitched her overall. 'Not very good. Not like Mr Parker's. What I thought of was: "Puffballs in fields is poisonous but out of packets is delicious."'

There was a puzzled silence.

'Er . . . what exactly . . . ?' William groped for an explanation without wishing to appear completely nonplussed.

'There's these things grow in fields, see, like mushrooms,' explained Mrs Fosdyke, quite pink with the interest she was creating. 'Look a bit like mushrooms, but if you was to eat them they'd kill you, you'd die in agony, my ma used to tell me. Fact is, I look at every mushroom I cook, I do, to be on the safe side. So you see I thought my slogan would be quite a good one, to let people know it wasn't *that* kind of puffball.'

'Mmmmm. Yes.' William tried to sound enthusiastic but came nowhere near it. 'I don't think that would have got you far, though. Too long, for one thing. And I don't think the breakfast cereal people would want the word "poisonous" in their adverts.'

'But they're not poisonous!' cried Mrs Fosdyke. 'That's the whole point!'

10

'Anyway, it was a good try,' Jack told her. 'I don't think I could have thought of that.'

'Oh well!' She shrugged and turned back to the sink. 'I don't pretend to be clever.'

She began to rattle dishes, which she could do with the best.

'I'll go and do my violin practice, I think,' Rosie said.

William followed her, in a drifting kind of way, hands in his pockets. He had had this kind of look about him ever since the Danish au pair, Atlanta, had left the previous week. If his ears had been the drooping kind, like Zero's, they would have drooped.

'I am glad,' observed Uncle Parker, 'that I do not live in this house. Everybody is always doing something. Does anybody ever do nothing?'

'I do,' Jack told him. 'And Zero.'

'Of course. Good for you.'

'Not what they say,' said Jack glumly. 'Sometimes I wish that being a Prophet and Phenomenon had come off, even if it would've been hard work.'*

'Rubbish!' said Uncle Parker briskly. 'It would have made an old man of you. Where's Grandma?'

* See *Ordinary Jack*.

He wanted Grandma to know about his prize because she had a very low estimate of him. It had been very low indeed since the day, some five years previously, when he had run over Thomas, a cantankerous ginger tom who had, she declared, been the light of her life. He had been the light of no one else's, having been given to scratching, biting, and attacking from corners, and none of the other Bagthorpes held his extinction against Uncle Parker. Some of them actually thanked him for it.

Uncle Parker had a secret admiration for Grandma and wanted her good opinion, though he would never have admitted this.

'Grandma's sitting in the dining-room,' Jack told him. 'She's feeling low and talking about Signs again. She's going on about her Birthday Portrait and all that.'

At Grandma's Birthday Party the whole table had gone up in flames and burnt out the dining-room before the fire brigade got there. One of the first things to go up had been Rosie's Birthday Portrait of Grandma, and ever since Grandma had taken this as a Sign, and thought it showed that the Fates, in some indefinable way, had it in for her. Every now and then she would go and sit on her own in the devastated dining-room and brood about this.

'I'll go and cheer her up,' said Uncle Parker.

'You'll only go and remind her of Thomas,' said Jack, 'and make her worse.'

'It's my belief,' remarked Mrs Fosdyke, who put her spoke into the wheels of anyone's conversation if she felt like it, 'that Mrs Bagthorpe Senior is too drawn into herself.'

'Drawn into herself, you reckon?' said Uncle Parker.

'All that Breathing, for one thing,' went on Mrs Fosdyke, encouraged by the interest in her diagnosis. 'It's time she stopped Breathing and went in for something else. Something that'd take her out of herself more.'

It occurred to Jack that if Grandma *were* to stop breathing, she would most certainly be taken out of herself—permanently. He knew, however, that what was being alluded to was not the common or garden kind of breathing that keeps people alive, but the kind of Breathing she had been doing daily since she had read one of Mrs Bagthorpe's books about yoga.

'What sort of thing had you in mind, Mrs Fosdyke?' asked Uncle Parker.

Mrs Fosdyke, hugely flattered by the unaccustomed interest being shown in her opinions, turned from the sink and wiped her hands on her pinafore.

'What I think,' she opined, with the gravity of a Harley Street Man delivering a long-awaited diagnosis, 'is that Mrs Bagthorpe Senior should take up Bingo.'

'Bingo, by Jove!' Uncle Parker was not easily put off balance, but he was now.

'Should *what?*' said Jack incredulously.

Grandma was a notorious cheat at anything from Scrabble to Ludo. Sometimes, at the end of a game of dominoes, for instance, she would say that a domino with five pips on it had six on it, or even three, and would play it accordingly. She also, at Snakes and Ladders, moved her counter up snakes and ladders alike, and never came down anything. At Monopoly, if she saw funds were getting low, she would declare that the Bank had forgotten to pay her £200 for passing Go on the last five rounds, and would snatch two five-hundred-pound notes out of the bank before anyone could stop her. She got away with it by being so old and obstinate, and by being able to keep up an argument longer than anyone else. Mostly when the Bagthorpes wanted to play games they went into quiet corners to do it, out of her way.

Mrs Fosdyke had been with the Bagthorpes long enough to know about Grandma's cheating, but was clearly not unduly perturbed.

'She won't be *allowed* to cheat,' she said, shaking her head. 'It's not allowed.'

'She will,' said Jack. 'I bet she would.'

'Can't.' Mrs Fosdyke shook her head firmly. 'They check up, see.'

'She'd tell them they'd checked up wrong,' Jack said.

'You can't argue,' said Mrs Fosdyke. 'There's no arguing allowed. They're ever so strict.'

'I think that Grandma would like Bingo,' said Uncle Parker. 'You're absolutely right, Mrs Fosdyke. Spot on. The very thing.'

'I could take her along with me.' Mrs Fosdyke was enchanted. 'There's ever such big prizes— there's money, of course, and then there's dinner services and blankets and non-sticks and all sorts. My sister at Pinxton won the Jackpot two weeks back on the day when they all have a link-up over the telephone, and she won four hundred pound!'

'Crikey!' Jack was impressed. 'I wouldn't mind a go. Though I'm not much good at numbers.'

'Oh, you don't have to be that,' Mrs Fosdyke assured him. 'There's no skill. No adding up, or anything. But it does take you out of yourself, you see, and that's why I thought it'd be the very thing for Mrs Bagthorpe Senior.'

'I shall go and tell her this minute,' announced Uncle Parker. 'A million thanks, Mrs Fosdyke. An inspired thought.'

Mrs Fosdyke glowed.

'Come on, Zero,' said Jack, and followed Uncle Parker.

Grandma was sitting on one of the new chairs that had been bought following the fire, contemplating the scene before her. The builders had been in and done some replastering and replaced some burned-up window frames and floorboards, but the room still looked like something out of an Alfred Hitchcock film. Everywhere was blacked up and charred-looking, and tatters of curtain still dangled from the buckled brass poles. Grandma looked as if she were reliving her Birthday Party in all its awful detail.

'Hallo, Grandma,' said Uncle Parker cheerily. 'Nice day.'

She did not move her gaze.

'I know you by your voice,' she said. 'You ran over Thomas, that shining jewel of a cat. You cut him off in his glorious prime.'

'Sorry about that, Grandma.' Uncle Parker apologized for at least the hundredth time. 'I'd offer to get you another, but I knew he was irreplaceable.'

'He *was* irreplaceable,' said Grandma mournfully. 'No cat could equal him for beauty, grace, and gentleness.'

(This was a statement that needed challenging. Thomas had been ill-favoured to a degree, and inspired hate and terror in all who knew him. It was lucky that Mr Bagthorpe was not there to point all this out.)

'I think a lot about Reincarnation these days,' Grandma went on to herself. 'I like to think who I would like to be Reincarnated as. I can't decide. I am bound to say I would prefer not to be a Bagthorpe again. I should like to think I would be promoted to a Higher Plane.'

'Got a bit of a treat for you, Grandma,' said Uncle Parker, beavering away at the cheerfulness.

'Life is but a dream,' remarked Grandma vaguely.

'Like as the waves make to the pebbled shore
So do our moments hasten to their ends.'

Uncle Parker was clearly batting on a sticky wicket.

'Heard about my prize, Grandma?' he asked.

'What prize?' said Grandma. 'When you get old, you don't get prizes.'

'Ah!' Uncle Parker was triumphant. 'But you do! There's a way you could win prizes the whole time.'

'When I was a little child, I once won a bag of macaroons at a party,' said Grandma wistfully. 'Those days will never come again.'

'They will, Grandma,' said Jack. 'Honestly. That's what he's trying to tell you.'

'I love macaroons,' she said. She seemed, marginally, to be coming back from wherever she had been.

'What would you say,' asked Uncle Parker, 'to a blanket? Or some non-sticks, whatever they are, or a dinner service? What would you say to four hundred pounds?'

'Four hundred pounds? Where?' She was with them now all right.

'Yours for the winning,' Uncle Parker told her with sublime confidence. 'All you do, you play a game.'

'Oh, I like playing games,' Grandma said. 'I always win at games.'

Uncle Parker and Jack exchanged glances. Grandma was evidently right back on the ball again now, because she said:

18

'I have a natural aptitude for games.'

'You certainly have a natural aptitude for *winning* them,' conceded Uncle Parker. 'One way or another. I'm bound to say none of us are any match for you.'

'This game would be a new challenge, though, Grandma,' said Jack. This was a guileful statement. Grandma rarely could resist a challenge.

'Whatever it is,' she replied, 'I shall expect to win.'

'That's the spirit, Grandma!' Uncle Parker told her. 'So you're on, then? Bingo tonight, is it?'

'Bingo?' repeated Grandma. 'Is that a game? Why do the Parkinsons call their dog after a game? I thought it was a name for a dog.'

'Because it's a *good* game,' Uncle Parker told her. 'You'll find out. And by the way, I might as well just mention it—I've just won a cruise for two in the Caribbean. I won it writing a slogan for Sugar-Coated Puffballs.'

Grandma favoured him with a long stare.

'If it were not for you,' she said at length, 'that beautiful, shining Thomas would at this moment be crooning in my lap. The rain rains on the just and the unjust.'

Jack, while himself thinking very little of Uncle

Parker's winning slogan, none the less felt he deserved better than this.

'It was a national competition,' he told her. 'The odds against winning are hundreds of thousands to one. It was pretty good going.'

Grandma rose. She reached the door and turned back.

'Do not quote statistics at me,' she said. 'The odds against Thomas being killed in his prime in the drive of his own home were hundreds of thousands to one. He—' she pointed straight at Uncle Parker—'was the Fly in the Statistics.'

She swept out of the charred dining-room having had, as always, the last word.

Chapter 2

During the course of that day the pile of recent newspapers and periodicals that lay on a shelf in the sitting-room rapidly and invisibly levelled down to a mere handful of colour supplements.

The Bagthorpes quite often all got the same idea at the same time, and quite often did not say a word to one another, each imagining him or herself to be the sole recipient of the particular inspiration. Tess playing her oboe, Rosie her violin, and William his drums, had each been lacking in their usual total concentration. Visions of Caribbean isles and palm trees danced between them and their semiquavers. Each, in turn, began to think along the same lines.

Mrs Bagthorpe was in her room up to her ears in Problems and was not involved. Nor was Jack, who was in the meadow trying to train Zero to Beg, nor Grandma, who was in the kitchen cross-examining Mrs Fosdyke on the finer points of Bingo. Grandpa had gone away for a few days to play bowls. If he had been present he would certainly not have gone in for Competitions. He was a very Non-Competitive Man, and the younger generation of Bagthorpes got all their drive from Grandma's side of the family.

Mr Bagthorpe was in his study reflecting bitterly on the unfairness of life. That Uncle Parker, who to all appearances did nothing but sit around doing crosswords or else tear about the countryside putting the fear of God into old and young alike, should actually have won a Caribbean Cruise simply by doodling with a form, was something Mr Bagthorpe just could not take. He himself had already been sitting at his desk for nearly two hours and all he had done so far was tear up five false starts to a script he was supposed to be doing. He would not have minded so much if Uncle Parker had won the prize by putting the right famous eyes into famous faces, or guessing where a football ought to be on a photograph, or something of that nature. It would even have been a fruitful source of sarcasm.

But that Uncle Parker should have won a prize by using *words*, which were the tools of Mr Bagthorpe's own trade, and which he felt to be more or less his exclusive province, was a bitter blow. Nothing would do, he decided, but that he himself should win an even bigger and better prize with a shorter and better slogan.

He was not a man to sit around playing with ideas. The minute he got one, he acted on it. (The critics often described his scripts as '*monumentally single-minded*' or '*ruthlessly one track*'.) Mr Bagthorpe took these as compliments, and they may have been, of course.

'*Lear* is monumentally single-minded,' he would point out triumphantly. '*Othello* was ruthlessly one track. So was *Macbeth*.'

Mr Bagthorpe, then, abandoned his abortive script and went to the sitting-room to find any magazines that might be running Competitions. He had often noticed them in the past but had thought it beneath his dignity to enter them. He had also, like Jack, thought that nobody ever won them anyway. He was not pleased to find that the magazine shelf had already been rifled, and guessed immediately what was afoot. He did not much like the idea that his offspring were intending to win Competitions too. It was, he knew, possible that he would end up by being a runner-up to one of them—Tess in particular, who was very good with words.

He instantly resolved, therefore, to keep his own Competition Entering secret. He was sure he would win every one he entered, if everything was all square and above board, and he was not pipped by a member of his own family. If, however, the Competitions were rigged (as he felt sure some of them must be, viz. Uncle Parker's success) and he did not win, then he would avoid loss of face. Mr Bagthorpe was very bad at losing face.

He did get ideas, however, and had one now. Competitions did not appear only in newspapers and periodicals, they also appeared on the backs, tops, and insides of grocery packages and tins. Uncle Parker's own success had depended upon the top of a Sugar-Coated Puffball carton. He determined to raid the larder. This, he realized, depended on side-tracking Mrs Fosdyke, who was not easy to dodge because she darted hither and thither about the house all day with the rapidity and inconsequential tracking of a hedgehog. She could be in the bathroom one minute, a bedroom the next, and then back down the hall, following her own obscure method of housekeeping. He had to think of a way of keeping her out of the kitchen for at least ten minutes while he had a quick sort through the pantry.

He pondered this for some time. He hit upon a solution. It was a neat one—it killed two birds with one stone.

In the kitchen he found Mrs Fosdyke serving coffee to his wife, the only member of the family who appeared to be interested in it. The rest, he surmised, were holed up in their rooms hammering out Slogans.

'Mrs Fosdyke has just been telling me how she has kindly offered to take mother to Bingo tonight,' she greeted him.

'To *what?*' demanded Mr Bagthorpe incredulously.

'To Bingo, dear. It will take her out of herself. You know how drawn into herself she has become lately.'

'Laura,' said her husband, 'if mother so much as sets foot in a Bingo Hall there will be a riot. You know there will.'

'Nonsense, dear,' said Mrs Bagthorpe firmly. (She gave so much thought and time to other people's Problems that as far as possible she tried to pretend that those of her own family were not there, in the hope that they would go away.)

'My mother,' said Mr Bagthorpe, 'and she *is* my mother, and I think I know her as well as anyone ever could, is a congenital cheater at games. No'—

he held up a hand—'don't bother to deny it. You were present, I believe, last week, when she concealed the Q in her handbag because all the Us had already gone, at Scrabble?'

'Oh, she won't be able to cheat at Bingo, Mr Bagthorpe,' said Mrs Fosdyke positively. 'It's impossible. It's all done ever so fair and square and businesslike.'

'Is it?' Mr Bagthorpe threw himself into a chair and reached for his coffee. 'Think they've got it organized, do they?'

'Oh, they have,' she assured him. 'They'd never keep going, otherwise. It's got to be fair.'

'In that case,' he said, 'I prophesy—if you will excuse the expression—that whatever Bingo Hall you frequent will be closed down within the week. I also think it possible the police will become involved, and that there will be adverse publicity in the local papers. Probably'—pausing for a gulp of coffee—'in the Nationals.'

'Oh, go on, Mr Bagthorpe!' said Mrs Fosdyke skittishly.

'Henry, dear, you do exaggerate,' his wife told him. 'I think it will be the healthiest thing possible for mother to do.'

'Oh, it'll be healthy for her, all right,' he agreed.

'There's nothing sets mother up like an all-out row.'

'Well, let's just wait and see, shall we,' said Mrs Bagthorpe sensibly. 'And thank you so much, Mrs Fosdyke, for your kind offer. We're most grateful.'

'Ah, and that reminds me, Mrs T—Fosdyke,' said Mr Bagthorpe. He had been about to say 'Mrs Tiggywinkle' but stopped himself just in time. 'There's a little favour you might do for me, if you will.'

'Really?' She looked startled. Mr Bagthorpe hardly ever spoke to her at all, and had never in memory asked a favour. He looked at her quite a lot, and she did not much like the way he looked, but he almost never actually said anything.

'If you'll excuse Mrs Fosdyke, dear,' he said to his wife, 'I'd like her to pop down to the village shop for me. I'm in the middle of a very difficult patch with my script, you see, and there's some material I must have if I'm to get on.'

'Well . . . certainly I've no objection,' said his wife, 'if—?'

She looked enquiringly at Mrs Fosdyke who was already wiping her hands on her overall preparatory to taking it off. She was going to enjoy telling them in the shop that she was there on an urgent errand to get something for one of Mr Bagthorpe's TV scripts.

'What is it you're wanting?' she enquired.

'It may sound strange,' replied Mr Bagthorpe, 'but what I require are current copies of the following magazines: *Woman's Monthly*, *Mother and Home*, *Happy Families* . . .'

He rattled off half a dozen more magazines that he felt sure would be rich in Competitions. These he had selected a few minutes earlier from *The Writer's and Artist's Year Book*. They were none of them publications that were usually to be found at Unicorn House.

Mrs Fosdyke looked surprised by this but Mrs Bagthorpe did not.

'I need,' explained Mr Bagthorpe shamelessly, 'to get right inside the mind of the woman in the home. Into the mind of a woman such as yourself, for instance, Mrs Fosdyke.'

Mrs Fosdyke positively scooted for her coat and hat on receiving this gratifying intelligence. She told her cronies about it later in the Fiddler's Arms.

'He's doing one of his scripts about me,' she boasted. 'Said he wanted to get right inside my mind. Researching up on it at the moment.'

On being jealously reminded by one of her friends that she had always pronounced Mr Bagthorpe to be mad, she replied:

'It goes in patches, does madness. He's in one of his sane spells'—which covered the present situation nicely, and also gave her a loophole whereby she could revert to her former assessment of Mr Bagthorpe if necessary.

Mrs Bagthorpe finished her coffee and went back to her Problems. Mrs Fosdyke, armed with a five-pound note and strong bag, was scuttling towards the village, and the coast was clear.

Mr Bagthorpe took a pair of scissors and went into the pantry. The haul was rich beyond his wildest expectations. There seemed hardly a packet or tin that did not offer the possibility of desirable rewards from motor cars to thousands of pounds, from holiday bungalows to trips to the Greek Islands. (Mr Bagthorpe was particularly bent on winning this latter, because it had a lot more tone than a trip to the Caribbean.) There were eight tins whose wrappers carried entry forms for this particular prize, and he swiftly removed them all and stowed them in his pocket. The very next batch of tins promised a motor car and also some very attractive runners'-up prizes, ranging from stereo equipment to typewriters. These, too, were divested of their wrappers.

All in all Mr Bagthorpe was in the pantry for a full quarter of an hour. He returned to his study a happy man, every pocket stuffed with wrappers and box lids, and hours of enjoyable Slogan Slogging before him. He sorted his pickings into businesslike piles, fetched out a new notebook and prepared a record-keeping system. He made notes of how many bottle tops of certain products he would have to collect and send along with his entries. He wrote the closing date of each competition in red, and by lunchtime the ground was prepared. All that now remained was the actual solving and Slogan-making—the least part of the thing, it seemed to Mr Bagthorpe, who was not a modest man.

The house was full of Bagthorpes similarly engaged. Rosie was sucking her pencil over a Slogan for aftershave (made difficult by her uncertainty as to what this product was actually supposed to do). In the end she settled for 'You may be no saint, but X will make you feel good.' William was writing a letter in not more than five hundred words explaining why he would like a motor caravan, and Tess had already thought of three sure-fire Slogans for a shampoo, and was now deciding that the best was probably: 'You may be no saint, but you will have a halo' (which, given Rosie's effort, suggested a strong telepathic link between Bagthorpes simultaneously generating ideas).

Jack, meanwhile, was slack and happy in the meadow with his dog. Zero did not really seem to want to sit up and beg, even when Jack dangled his favourite biscuits above him. The reason Jack wanted him to learn was to increase his standing among the other Bagthorpes. Even now that he could fetch sticks, none of them really thought much of him. It was Mr Bagthorpe who had given him his name. 'If there was anything less than Zero, that hound would be it,' he had said. It was not a good name to have to go through life with, and Jack sometimes wondered if it affected Zero, and gave him an inferiority complex. He spent a lot of time trying to build up Zero's confidence, because he could tell by the way his ears drooped when he was getting sad and undermined.

This morning, for instance, after each unsuccessful attempt by Zero to beg, Jack had hurled a stick and shouted 'Fetch!' and each time Zero had brought it back he was patted and praised and given a biscuit.

At present Jack was having a rest and wondering how best to tackle the problem. He felt sure that Zero could sit up and beg if only he, Jack, found the key to how his mind worked.

He's got quite thick legs and a very square-shaped sort of bottom, he thought, so there's no *physical* reason why he can't beg. It must be all in the mind.

There was, of course, one obvious method Jack could use for getting through to Zero. He had been keeping it as a last resort, because the only other occasion he had used it was one of his most painful memories. It was the most embarrassing moment of his life. Jack had been trying to get through to Zero how to fetch sticks, and in the end had himself dropped down on all fours, crawled after the stick and picked it up in his own teeth. Mr Bagthorpe had caught him in the act. It had been terrible. The only thing was, it had worked.

And it could work again now, he thought. In fact, it's probably the only way.

Unfortunately the thing was not so simple as it seemed. He would need, he realized, an accomplice. Someone would have to hold up a biscuit for Jack to sit up and beg for. It would, he was convinced, be no use his holding up a biscuit for himself. This would only confuse Zero more than ever.

Jack slumped back into the grass.

That's it, then, he thought. He knew for a fact that none of his family was going to hold up a biscuit for Jack to beg for. He also knew that he would never ask them. They were all genii, and he was ordinary. To ask them to hold up biscuits would be to invite the fate of being *sub*-ordinary. He half shut his eyes and squinted through the long, seeding grass and saw the light running like wires. He heard Zero's steady panting by his ear, and was content. It was a shock to hear Uncle Parker's voice.

'Hallo, there. Having a kip?'

Jack shot up and shaded his eyes against the low autumn sun to stare up at his uncle, six foot four above ground level, and looking amused in the friendly way he had. Jack and Uncle Parker were old conspirators. They understood one another.

'Not kipping,' Jack told him. 'Just having a bit of a think.'

'Ah.' Uncle Parker sat down himself and pulled a grass to chew.

Jack explained the problem.

'Well,' said Uncle Parker when he had finished, 'here's your third party.'

'You? Would you?'

'No trouble. Nothing much to holding up biscuits. Got some handy?'

Jack indicated the bag containing the remainder.

'There's just one thing you might do for me,' Uncle Parker said.

'What?'

'Go to the Bingo place with Grandma and Fozzy. I'll give you a sub. Can't let that pair loose on their own.'

Jack saw his point. He knew that Grandma was going to cheat, and that when she was found out she would need protecting. Mrs Fosdyke was not the protecting type. She would probably scuttle like a rat off a sinking ship the minute the police arrived. (Jack, like Mr Bagthorpe, felt sure that the kind of cheating Grandma would go in for would eventually involve the police.)

'I'll do it,' he said. 'I'll go. Might even win.'

'Could easily,' agreed Uncle Parker. 'Pure chance. No skill. No offence.'

'Come on, then,' Jack said. 'Let's start the training. Here.'

He handed up the bag of biscuits. He himself then crouched on all fours beside Zero, who was dozing.

'Hey, Zero!'

34

Zero opened his eyes and his ears picked up slightly.

'Now—watch me!'

Zero yawned hugely and moved to a sitting position. He looked dazed.

'Now,' whispered Jack to Uncle Parker, 'you say "Up!" and I'll sit up and beg. If I do it and he doesn't, you say "Good boy!" and pat my head, and give me the biscuit.'

Uncle Parker nodded. He delved in the bag and came up with a chocolate digestive which he broke in half.

'Right.'

He held the biscuit aloft halfway between Jack and Zero.

'Up. Sit up. Beg. Good boy—boys, rather.'

Jack accordingly crouched on his legs and held his hands drooping forward in imitation of front paws.

'Good *boy*!' exclaimed Uncle Parker. He patted Jack on the head and held out the biscuit. Jack opened his mouth and Uncle Parker pushed the half digestive into it. It nearly choked him. He looked sideways to see that Zero was looking distinctly interested. For one thing, his eyes were fixed soulfully on the piece of biscuit still protruding from Jack's mouth, and for another, he was doing a kind of stamping movement with his front paws alternately, like a race horse impatient to be loosed.

'Look!' The exclamation came out with a shower of crumbs. 'Look at his paws!'

Uncle Parker nodded.

'We're on the right track. All we've got to do now is keep on reinforcing the message. How hungry are you?'

'Not terribly,' Jack told him. 'You could break the biscuits in quarters instead of halves. They'll last longer that way.'

The training session continued. It was going well. Uncle Parker and Jack became increasingly pleased with themselves and increasingly entertained by Zero's efforts to raise himself with his front paws up. He had very big, furry paws— pudding-footed, Mr Bagthorpe called him—and he did not seem to have much control over them. Once or twice he toppled over sideways within an ace of success and rolled about growling with annoyance.

'I wish we'd got a camera,' Jack said. 'I've never seen anything so funny.' He then added immediately, for the benefit of Zero's ears, 'And it's jolly good the way he's catching on. You're nearly there, old chap. Good old boy. Good boy.'

He was the only Bagthorpe who ever praised Zero and he had to do a lot of it to keep his confidence and his ears up.

Had Jack known it, a camera was in the offing. It was going to be used at any moment, just as soon as Rosie could stop stuffing her fists into her mouth to keep herself from giggling out loud, and use her hands to operate the camera instead.

Rosie was behind a hawthorn bush not six feet from where the training was taking place. The reason why she was there was because she was out to get some shots for a Competition entitled 'Me and My Pet'. At first she had passed it over, because she did not have a pet. She was too busy with her maths and violin and Portraits and swimming (which were the four main Strings to her Bow) to have time for a pet. She had then, however, thought of Jack and Zero. She turned back to the Competition and discovered that what was really wanted was something unusual.

One of the most unusual things Rosie had ever heard of (she had, to her intense annoyance, missed actually seeing it) was Jack on all fours with a stick in his mouth to show Zero how to Fetch. She had afterwards begged him to repeat the performance so that she could photograph it with her new camera. Rosie had a passion for keeping records of things so strong that it could almost have been classed as a fifth String to her Bow. She had even offered Jack her spare pocket calculator to pose like this, but he always refused point blank.

'You do it,' he told her, 'and I'll photograph *you* doing it.'

'No,' she said. 'I'd look silly.'

'There you are, then. Anyway, it wasn't silly, even if it looked it. It was a Serious Scientific Experiment, and it worked.'

Rosie was now poised ready to take a shot—more than one, if possible—of the present Serious Scientific Experiment which was funnier, definitely, than the first could possibly have been. A 16mm movie camera complete with tripod, screen, and projector were as good as in the bag.

'Hold up half a digestive this time,' she heard Jack tell Uncle Parker. 'He's about there. I'm sure he is. They're one of his favourites.'

Uncle Parker took the biscuit and poised it between the pair of them.

'Up!' he commanded. 'Sit up! Beg!'

Jack went through his usual motions, turned his

head sideways and saw that Zero too, though rocking alarmingly, was up, tongue dangling, eyes fixed on the digestive.

No one heard the click of Rosie's shutter because of Zero's panting. Solemnly Uncle Parker placed the biscuit in Zero's jaws.

'Good *boy*,' he said, and Jack scrambled up and began patting Zero so vigorously that he spluttered crumbs. Behind her bush, Rosie secretly thanked them all.

'Oh, it worked, it worked!' Jack cried. 'Oh thanks, Uncle Parker! I'd never've done it without you. Oh, wait till the rest of them see!'

Uncle Parker was looking more thoughtful than jubilant.

'Interesting . . .' he murmured.

He was thinking of Daisy, who needed training as much as Zero did—probably more. He was wondering whether he could adopt this kind of technique to deal with her and make her less of a public nuisance. It was true that she did not light fires any more, but Mr Bagthorpe had not been far short of the mark when he had suggested that she was now poisoning people. She was, among other things, going into the pantry and mixing all kinds of things together, like cocoa and gravy salt, for instance, and salt and sugar, and marmalade and chutney. The Parkers and their friends had been getting some truly horrible gastronomic shocks of late.

Aunt Celia did not take this very seriously, partly because she was a vegetarian and lived mainly on lettuce, carrots, wheatgerm, and fresh orange juice. She said that it showed signs of creativity, Daisy's mixing ingredients together.

'It is one of the early signs of creative genius,' she said, in an unusually long sentence for her, 'to Reconcile the Seemingly Disparate.'

Uncle Parker did not dispute this. For one thing, he never argued with his wife because he thought she was perfect. Also, she had a very highly strung temperament and must not be crossed. He had put a padlock on the pantry door, however, saying that if Daisy were as creative as all that, she would find other Disparate objects to Reconcile.

The trouble was, she had. Daisy had embarked on a career of Reconciling the Seemingly Disparate that was shortly to drive the Bagthorpe household to the edge of their endurance while the Parkers were in the Caribbean. Anybody else would have gone right over the edge.

Meanwhile, Uncle Parker made a mental note

to try the Zero technique on his daughter on his return, and dismissed the matter from his mind.

'I think we ought to do it again, once or twice,' Jack said. 'Just to make absolutely sure he's got it.'

Rosie, behind her hawthorn, hugged herself and wound her film on. All in all, she got five shots of the repeat beggings. As it turned out, her film and the supply of biscuits ran out together. She remained under cover while Uncle Parker and Jack sauntered over the meadow back towards the house.

Zero followed, his ears at an unusually jaunty angle. Perhaps he had a deep, canine intuition that before long he was going to be the most famous, most photographed, most sought after dog in England, if not indeed the world.

Better still, he was about to show Mr Bagthorpe who was Zero and who was not.

Chapter 3

The natural misgivings about Grandma setting off to Bingo with Mrs Fosdyke that evening were not so deeply felt as they might ordinarily have been. The Bagthorpes had something else to think about. They had nearly all added Competition Entering as an Extra String to their respective Bows, and were involved in it as obsessively and singlemindedly as only the Bagthorpes knew how to be. At this stage, each of them suspected what the others were up to but no one could be sure exactly what, so that there was a strong air of guerrilla warfare about the place too.

It was unlucky for Jack and Zero that the rest of the family were so preoccupied, because it meant that Zero's new feat did not receive due recognition and applause.

'What? Oh, he can do that, can he?' was all Mr Bagthorpe had said at lunchtime. 'Well, he needn't do it at me.'

'I don't think we want that at table, dear,' was Mrs Bagthorpe's only contribution.

The only member of the family who seemed unstintedly happy and admiring was Rosie, gleeful in the knowledge that her camera held film of what must surely be the most unusual 'Me and My Pet' shots ever taken. So warm was she in her admiration, so many pieces of meat did she hold up for Zero to take, that Jack, had he been of a suspicious nature, must surely have been suspicious. The Bagthorpes respected one another's achievements but did not usually wax lyrical about them. They saved the lyricism for their personal successes.

The one good thing about the lukewarm reception of Zero's latest String to his Bow was that no one bothered to ask Jack how it had been achieved. He did not really want to describe how it had been done, and felt certain Uncle Parker would not want this information bandied about either.

Grandma had gone to have lunch and spend the afternoon at Mrs Fosdyke's, whose half day it was. The pair of them had gone off looking uncommonly pleased with themselves. They had never been friends before, and it seemed odd to see them trotting down the drive together, Mrs Fosdyke with her black plastic carrier and Grandma wearing her fur coat (though it was unseasonably warm for October) and carrying an umbrella. Mr Bagthorpe had his misgivings about the latter accessory.

'If she doesn't win,' he said, 'and she won't, she'll end up laying about her with that umbrella. You mark my words.'

None of the others had said anything in reply because it occurred to them that Mr Bagthorpe could be right about this.

'The only safe game for her to play,' he went on, 'is Patience.' (Grandma did play Patience, for hours on end sometimes, and it came out every time.)

Jack was due to meet the two ladies at the bus stop at a quarter past six to escort them to the Bingo Hall in Aysham. Mrs Fosdyke did not usually play there, and was nervous at the prospect. She usually played at a small hall in the next village of Maythorpe. But there were games there only on Wednesdays and Saturdays. Today was Tuesday, and Grandma, once fired by an idea, did not care to be held up by even twenty-four hours.

On the bus Mrs Fosdyke confided in them that what was really worrying about the hall in Aysham was that it was so big.

'Used to be an old theatre, you see,' she told

them. 'Holds hundreds. What I'm afraid is, that if I shout "Bingo!" they won't hear.'

'I shall shout with you,' Grandma told her. 'I shall shout and attract attention by waving my umbrella.'

Jack winced. Uncle Parker had given him a pound to play with, but he was now beginning to feel that even if he won the Jackpot it was going to be a high price to pay for sitting next to Grandma at a game she would almost certainly lose.

'Another thing, of course,' went on Mrs Fosdyke, 'there's a lot more people. Makes the prizes better, of course, but you don't stand the same chance of winning.'

'*I* shall win,' said Grandma with decision.

The hall was certainly very big and had a lot of gilt moulding and red plush about it. Grandma approved of this decor. She said it 'took her back'. They arrived five minutes before the start of play and the hall was already three-quarters full. Mrs Fosdyke spent the time giving Grandma last-minute coaching on how to mark her card.

'And remember,' she told her, 'there's a small prize for getting a line, up, down, or across, or all four corners. But to get the big prize, you have to get the whole lot.'

'I see,' said Grandma happily. 'Is he going to begin?'

Now Grandma had had it explained a hundred times during the course of the day that this was one game she could not hope to win every time. She had been told it tactfully and tactlessly, gently and rudely. She had been told that it was quite possible that she would not win a single game during the course of the evening. She had not replied to any of this, but she had worn a certain look on her face. It was the look that meant that whatever was being said to her was like water off a duck's back.

None the less, Jack had expected Grandma to stay the course longer than the first game. He knew she would not stand for losing many games, but he had expected her to stand for losing one.

He was wrong. Grandma came nowhere near winning the first game because for one thing she said the microphone was too loud for her to hear clearly. She was also confused by the 'legs eleven' and 'two little ducks' and 'sixty-six clickety click' aspect of things. Mrs Fosdyke had told her some of them, but not all, and it really did hold her back.

Everyone else there seemed to be an old hand.

They were poised over their boards, some of them playing two or more at a time and flashing their hands about with the speed of light. Grandma was seventy-five and sometimes she got rheumatism in her hands, and even when she did get a number it took her so long to deal with it that she missed the next one.

She then poked Mrs Fosdyke and hissed 'What—what was that? Clickety what?' with the result that both she and Mrs Fosdyke missed the next number after that as well. Jack himself was doing quite well, and was only one number short when the first line was called.

The woman who won it was on the row in front, further along, and Grandma glowered at her innocent back.

'Ridiculous!' she snapped. 'I've only five numbers on my whole card yet. Isn't he going to do something about it?'

'Sometimes they *do* win quick,' said Mrs Fosdyke, whispering in the hope that Grandma would lower her voice too.

'I thought you said there was no cheating allowed?' Grandma said loudly and distinctly.

'There *isn't*!' hissed poor Mrs Fosdyke. People were beginning to look at them. 'Sshh—he's

47

starting again—you might win the whole game yet.'

Grandma did not win the whole game, though it was not for want of trying. She adopted the tactic, whenever she did not hear a number properly, of marking off one of her numbers at random anyway. She probably thought this was fair. There was no vice in Grandma. It was simply that she couldn't stand losing.

The second game was about to get under way when Grandma rose in her seat. Jack shrivelled inside his skin.

'Young man!' she called. 'Young man!'

The caller, a balding man wearing a cream jacket and red-spotted bow tie, glanced about looking puzzled. Grandma picked up her umbrella and waved it.

'Here!' she called. 'Here, young man!'

He placed her, and said into his microphone: 'What's up, then, madam?'

'Would you mind not talking into that loud-speaker thing,' called Grandma. 'I can hear you much better without it.'

A murmuring broke out in the hall, and it was getting increasingly difficult for anyone to hear anything.

'Ssshh!' hissed the caller into his microphone, and his clients immediately stopped their chatter.

'I simply want to say,' Grandma told him, in her clear, ringing tones, 'that I am not likely to win this game the way it is being played at present.'

A deathly hush settled on the hall. Nothing like this had ever happened before, nothing remotely like it. Sometimes the odd drunk would get up and start shouting and have to be hustled out, but Grandma obviously did not fall into this category.

'To begin with,' she said, 'I would rather you did not use that loudspeaker. If you just call the numbers loudly and distinctly in your normal voice, as I am speaking now, it will be quite sufficient.'

The bald man's mouth was slightly ajar now.

'The next thing is,' she resumed, 'that I would like you, please, to refrain from adding these peculiar "clickety clacks" and "doctor's orders" to the numbers you call. We were not taught our numbers like this when I was at school. Also, I am only a learner, and I am not familiar with them. I am perfectly familiar with the numbers up to a hundred, however, and if you would kindly call them in an undecorated form, I think I shall do very well.'

She paused. The caller looked as if he thought

he was having a nightmare, aghast and astounded at the same time, and when his mouth started to move, at first no sound came out. At last he managed, very faintly:

'Is that all?'

'I think so,' said Grandma. 'Oh—there is one more small point. I am, as I have told you, a beginner. Until I have had a little more practice I would appreciate it if you could call the numbers more slowly. I think you are going too fast. Possibly others here feel the same?'

She looked enquiringly about her and met with total non-confirmation. The regulars gaped back at her with blank, stunned faces.

'Perhaps those who do feel the same, would like to raise their right hands?' she suggested. No one moved. Jack noticed that two large men in uniforms had appeared at either end of the row where they were sitting. They would, he realized with horror, bundle Grandma out at a nod from the caller.

Over my dead body, he thought, and tried not to imagine the details.

On the rostrum there were signs that the caller was beginning to collect himself.

'I must apologize for this interruption, ladies and gentlemen,' he said into the microphone.

'Oh, and do accept my own apologies, too,' chipped in Grandma. 'I think I have said all that I wanted to say. Thank you.'

She sat down. She looked almost as if she expected a round of applause. She was the only person in the whole hall who looked pleased with herself. The regulars were beginning to murmur again.

'If we are all ready, then,' said the caller, 'we'll start the next game. Eyes down for the lucky winner of another sensational prize. And the first number—wait for it—all the fives, fifty-five.'

Jack numbly crossed this off his own card and waited for the inevitable. The caller, he realized, was going to carry on as if the interruption had never occurred. He was going to pretend Grandma had never spoken. And Jack knew that when Grandma was anywhere, people *knew* she was. She was not ignorable. To a point he could sympathize with the man. He was probably not, he reflected, very bright. He certainly had not been able to think of a single word to say in reply to Grandma. But then, if he spent every day of his life calling out numbers, perhaps he was not very good with words any more. Perhaps he had lost his conversation.

What Grandma did next was the worst thing

she could possibly have done. Her big mistake was not realizing that every single person in that hall took this game at least as seriously as she herself. They were all obviously better losers (they could not be worse) but they were all playing to win. Tension builds up very high in a Bingo Hall after even the first few numbers have been called. If only Grandma had sat and sulked till the game was over, and then stood up and said her piece, the worst that could have happened was that she would have been asked to leave. She might even have got her money back at the door.

As it was, she came very near getting lynched. She, Mrs Fosdyke, and Jack could all have got lynched. She stood up, right in the middle of a call of 'Lucky for some—thirteen!' and shouted 'Stop!' at the top of her considerable voice.

'Sit down!' and 'Shut up!'—these, and other less politely phrased requests and exclamations came from all parts of the hall. Several of the players themselves stood up and waved their arms while making their protests and thus set other people off doing the same thing and within thirty seconds flat everyone in there had, with the exception of the halt and the lame, got on his or her feet yelling. The caller was yelling too, into his microphone, but yelling must have affected its vibrations because you couldn't hear the words at all, only a kind of booming. It was probably as well.

From then on, everything happened more or less as Mr Bagthorpe had predicted it would. A riot broke out. The interesting thing was, and Jack could not help noticing this at the time, that although people started hurling abuse and even hitting one another, nobody did this to Grandma herself. Standing there with her umbrella aloft in the manner of the Statue of Liberty, she seemed in some curious way to be above it all, even though it was she who had set the whole thing off.

Somebody obviously panicked and rang the police, and they arrived quickly, about ten of them, and gradually quietened people down. The bald-headed caller was still booming into his microphone and making gestures with his hands as if tearing at the hair he had once had. When everyone else had sat down quietly under the watchful eyes of the police he sounded suddenly very silly, booming like that, and stopped abruptly.

In the ensuing silence the people on Grandma's row stood up quite politely and let the trio pass to the gangway, and they were escorted out of the hall by two policemen. In the foyer one of them, a sergeant, took out a notebook.

'Now then,' he said, 'what's it all about?'

'It wasn't Grandma's fault,' said Jack instantly.

'Oh, I don't know, officer, I really don't know!' Mrs Fosdyke, incredibly, was close to tears. 'I shouldn't never have brought her.'

'I think perhaps we'd better go along to the station,' said the sergeant.

He gave certain orders to the constable, who went back into the hall. Grandma, Mrs Fosdyke, and Jack walked in silence to the swing doors. Several police cars were standing out there, one with its blue light flashing.

Grandma had gone very quiet and dignified. Mrs Fosdyke kept sniffing all the way to the station. Jack was torn between enjoyment of being in the novel situation of riding as an apprehended criminal in a police car, and a sinking feeling that he had let Uncle Parker and everybody else down.

At the station Grandma kept up her silent dignity for a while, but after a cup of tea seemed to thaw and consented to give her version of what had transpired. She stood up.

'I solemnly swear that all I shall say will be the truth, the whole truth, and nothing but the truth, so help me God,' she began. 'Shouldn't I have a Bible to hold while I say that?'

'Oh, there's no call for that at all, madam,' the sergeant told her. 'Not at this stage.'

'I think I have seen enough television films about policemen and criminals,' Grandma told him, 'to know something of procedure. I suppose I should not be surprised that the Bible is no longer required. It is yet another sign of the times.'

In the end she gave a very good account, Jack thought. And when she told what she had said to the Bingo man, and the requests she had made, they all sounded very reasonable, and nothing like riot-raising speeches. Jack could tell from the policemen's faces that they were thinking this too.

'First time you'd played, then, was it, Mrs Bagthorpe?' asked one of them. 'I can see how it must have been confusing.'

'Precisely,' she nodded. 'I simply thought that some consideration should be shown to a beginner. And I thought that young man very rude indeed when he just carried on as if I had never spoken.'

All in all, the interview went very well. At the end of the day, it was clear that the only word Grandma had spoken which could be even loosely interpreted as riot-raising and provocative, was the single word 'Stop!', and even Jack could see that this would not stand up very well in Court.

In the end Grandma was told that no charges would be preferred though she was advised to avoid Bingo halls in future. It appeared that two witnesses had also been interviewed, and their version of what happened had corresponded almost exactly with her own, except that they had added that Grandma was, in their view, mad.

The whole thing was just beginning to be rather enjoyable when the police asked whom they might telephone to take the trio home. Grandma gave their number, and Jack shut his eyes and prayed that Mr Bagthorpe would not answer the phone. He did. Jack could hear, even from where he was sitting, the snapped out 'Well?' which was the way his father always let people know he was being interrupted doing something important on one of his scripts. (In this particular instance, as it happened, he had been on the verge of a Slogan that was going to win him a new car and a thousand pounds to spend on petrol.)

From what the police said after the telephone call Jack gathered that Mr Bagthorpe had come much nearer being prosecuted than Grandma ever had. He created a good deal of sympathy for

Grandma, and she was further plied with cups of tea. The police thought they could see why she was driven out to play Bingo at nights.

With the Bagthorpes, when things were bad they inevitably tended to go to worse. The long day was not yet over. When Mr Bagthorpe arrived he was in a very bad temper. He immediately set in on the police for what he called the 'malicious persecution of an innocent and elderly lady'—which might have been interpreted as a gallant gesture, but was not.

Neither the police (who had been very kind indeed) nor Grandma (who did not like being described as 'elderly') thanked him for it. He would, as it turned out, have been wiser to play the scene in a much lower key.

It did not escape the attention of a very junior constable that Mr Bagthorpe's road fund licence was a month out of date. For this he was duly booked. Grandma could have put in a word for him, because she had gone down very well with the police, but she evidently did not choose to.

During the silence that prevailed in the car on the way home, the only words spoken were spoken by Grandma herself, and had been carefully chosen for their ambiguity.

'Truth,' she observed in the darkness and silence, 'will speak out of stone walls.'

No one replied.

Chapter 4

It might reasonably have been supposed that the day following the Bingo debacle would have been a quiet one, even something of an anticlimax. That had been the kind of day that is difficult to match. Some families never have a day like it in their lives.

Mrs Fosdyke was in two minds whether to take the day off. She felt this would be justifiable in view of the hammering her nervous system had taken the previous night. On the other hand, Mr Bagthorpe was doing a script about her and trying to get inside her mind. When it came on television, she did not want her mind to appear in a bad light. Some people might call it weak to take days off for nervous reasons. In the end she decided to go, but not until midmorning. She was later to regret coming in at all.

Things were not too bad to begin with. All the Bagthorpes were much entertained by the account of what had happened at Bingo. Grandma herself was not the least cast down. She enjoyed winning games, but she also enjoyed a good free-for-all, and in this respect had had more than her money's worth. The only person present at breakfast who was not in high spirits was Mr Bagthorpe, who was still sore about his humiliating encounter with the police. He maintained that if there was a fine, Grandma should pay it. He further went on to say that if anybody's licence got endorsed it should be hers, and that it was his luck that she should not possess one.

'I carry the can for everybody,' he declared. 'I'm the Archetypal Can-carrier of all time.'

'It is illegal to go about with an out-of-date licence,' Grandma told him piously. 'And at your age, you should know that, Henry.'

'I hadn't even noticed,' he replied. 'If it had been five *years* out of date I should not have noticed. Or five hundred years. I have my mind on higher things.'

'You might try explaining that to the police,' said Grandma. 'But it does not sound like a convincing argument to me, and I doubt whether it will to them. They, after all, are not even your mother.'

After breakfast the Bagthorpes retired to their rooms for a short period and then, one by one, made trips into the village, to the Post Office. They needed things like stamps and Postal Orders in connection with the Competition Entering. They bought some magazines too, after having had a quick leaf through to make sure they had any Competitions worth entering. Some of these were the same ones as Mrs Fosdyke had fetched for Mr Bagthorpe the day before.

It was around midmorning that things began to hot up. First of all Uncle Parker came round to find out how Grandma had got on at Bingo. Grandma was just finishing her account when Mr Bagthorpe entered the kitchen, having smelt coffee.

'Oh bad *luck*, Henry,' Uncle Parker greeted him. 'Would you believe it! Well, that's one thing I've never had, I'm happy to say—an endorsement.'

This made Mr Bagthorpe genuinely feel like murdering Uncle Parker. He clenched and unclenched his hands and it was nearly a full minute before he trusted himself to speak.

'If there were any justice,' he said '—and there isn't—you would not have anything so trivial as an endorsement. You would long ago have been banned from driving for life, and possibly even imprisoned.'

Here Grandma was inclined to agree.

'That is perfectly true,' she said. 'At least you, Henry, never ran over a beautiful and innocent cat.'

'Quite,' said Mr Bagthorpe, letting this inaccurate description of Thomas go. 'Nor was I, I'm happy to say, responsible for encouraging a sheltered old lady to run loose in a Bingo hall.'

He had gone too far.

'Just one moment,' said Grandma frigidly. 'Is it to myself you are alluding as a "sheltered old lady"? If so, I take the utmost exception to the expression. I am not sheltered—nobody who has lived in this house all the years I have could ever be sheltered. And I am not old.'

'Of course not.' Uncle Parker saw his chance of winning her back on his side. 'Age cannot wither you nor the years condemn, nor custom stale your infinite variety.'

This complicatedly worded compliment set off a heated argument about mixed sources. Mr Bagthorpe maintained that half of it was from a poem about the war dead, by Binyon, and the other half from *Antony and Cleopatra*. Uncle Parker, realizing he was right, sidestepped by saying that he had been perfectly aware of this. It was an impromptu remark, he said, and without wishing to boast, it was a sign of creative genius to Reconcile the Seemingly Disparate.

This inflamed Mr Bagthorpe still further, and a real three-cornered fight was just getting under way when Mrs Fosdyke, whom everyone had been ignoring, suddenly let out a wild shriek. The row stopped dead. A lot of shrieking went on in the Bagthorpe house, but to date none of it had come from Mrs Fosdyke.

They all turned. She was standing in the doorway of the pantry looking pale and distraught. In each hand she held out a tin without a label.

'There's thousands of them!' she shrieked. 'And tops off packets and holes in the sides of things!'

Only Mr Bagthorpe among those present had the faintest idea what she was talking about. He wished himself at the ends of the earth, the salt-mines.

Mrs Fosdyke let the tins fall and watched them dully as they rolled away over the tiles. She turned back, picked up two more tins and let them go the same way. Jack thought it obvious that she had gone mad, like Ophelia, but instead of strewing flowers was rolling tins. They all stood there and watched till the tins finally came to rest. There was a silence. The next words clearly had to be spoken by Mrs Fosdyke, and they waited patiently. She started off by shaking her head. She shook her head for quite a long time and then at last spoke, but not really to them, more to herself.

'Plums and haricots, beans and tomatoes,' she intoned. She repeated it, as if it were a line of poetry. 'Plums and haricots, beans and tomatoes.'

Still no one else spoke. There seemed no answer to this kind of remark. After another pause she elaborated on her theme.

'Pineapple and mince, a dozen of cling peaches there was. Which is what, and whatever else?'

Mrs Fosdyke really did sound poetic as never before. She sounded like the Fool in *Lear*, rather. She turned back into the pantry and lifted two large packets and held them out. They were Sugar-Coated Puffballs. The tops of both had been torn off. Again she wagged her head.

'Who?' she asked, half to herself. 'Who would ever? And why? What have I done? What can it mean?'

She paused after asking these five questions, and seemed to be casting around herself for an answer.

'Aha!' Jack heard Uncle Parker exclaim softly. 'I think I see the light.'

'I should've stopped at home,' mourned Mrs Fosdyke. 'I nearly never came. Not after last night.'

'What was wrong with last night?' demanded Grandma instantly. She had not been very interested in the tin rolling and poetry, particularly as it had interrupted a good argument. 'I enjoyed last night.'

'I've never been in trouble with the police,' went on Mrs Fosdyke. 'Never. And now this. I can't carry on.'

'Nonsense!' Grandma told her briskly. 'Jack, pick up those tins. Why are you rolling tins, Mrs Fosdyke?'

'Beans, peaches, tomatoes, plums. All sorts.'

'Somebody,' observed Uncle Parker, 'is going in for Competitions. Somebody, Mrs F., has been removing labels and lids from your pantry to send off with Competitions.'

'Not me,' said Jack promptly. He surfaced, holding the tins, caught sight of his father's face, and saw the truth written on it.

'The whole family's going in for Competitions,' blustered Mr Bagthorpe. He didn't care who found out about this so long as Uncle Parker never did. 'It's you that started it with that wretched Caribbean thing.' He had evidently decided that

65

attack might be the best form of defence. Another row would act as a smokescreen.

'Which brand of cling peaches is it, I wonder,' mused Uncle Parker, 'that could be offering a month in the saltmines?'

'Luckily, my salt's all right,' soliloquized Mrs Fosdyke dismally, off on her own again. 'And my sugar. And my marmalades and jams is all right I suppose even without labels. It's my tins. You can't see through tins.'

This was incontestable. As they stood and pondered the matter Mrs Bagthorpe came in and pieced the story together and went into the pantry to inspect the damage.

'*Everyone* will have Sugar-Coated Puffballs at breakfast now,' she announced, 'until they are all used up. We must eat them before they go soft. Some of us could have them for supper as well. When we find out who is responsible for this irresponsible act, then that person will probably be required to eat Sugar-Coated Puffballs at every meal. It would have a certain poetic justice.'

'But the tins!' wailed Mrs Fosdyke. 'What about my tins?'

What happened about the tins was to affect the Bagthorpes' lives, and particularly their eating habits, for a long time to come. Meals could no longer be counted on in the way they once could. The family had never before, for instance, eaten processed peas with custard. Nor did they now, for that matter. But Mrs Bagthorpe had ruled that whatever tin was opened, its contents must be consumed, so they ate the peas first, then the custard separately afterwards. This particular combination came up quite often, because the sound of a tin of processed peas when shaken was practically indistinguishable from that of raspberries or prunes or fruit salad.

All the Bagthorpes took up Tin Shaking, and there would be fearful rows at first. William maintained that the tins could be identified by an elimination method, but his identification record was as bad as anyone else's. He was particularly bad at distinguishing between condensed soup and rice pudding, and the family often found themselves ending a meal with soup having started it in the same way. Sometimes they even got the same flavour. They were really furious with William when this happened.

In the end it was decided that a rota should be drawn up, and each Bagthorpe in turn should Shake a Tin, and try to produce the commodity Mrs

Fosdyke required. Being Bagthorpes, they could not, of course, leave it at this, and developed a scoring system which was pinned on the pantry door next to the rota. Points were awarded from One to Five, depending on the accuracy of the guess.

You could only score Five by being dead accurate—in the case of soup, say, you actually had to produce the required flavour. Nobody got Five very often. Four was awarded to a near miss, such as raspberries for strawberries, and Three to successfully producing the right category, i.e. fruit as opposed to soup or savoury. Two was for a tin of tomatoes (Mrs Fosdyke had been hoarding them for months and one's chance of picking them out was at least five to one) and One point went to asparagus, which the Bagthorpes adored, and did not mind eating even at breakfast, following the mandatory Sugar-Coated Puffballs.

For anything not in any of these five categories you simply scored nothing, with the sole exception that if you opened processed peas at breakfast you got five deducted. William actually went to the lengths of buying a tin of peas from the village shop, so that he could compare how it sounded when shaken, but this created violent opposition and was ruled out of order.

Grandpa was put in the rota at his own request. He had great confidence in his new hearing aid (he had lost the old one in Grandma's Birthday Party Fire) and it must have been fairly effective because his scoring was more or less on a par with everyone else's.

The Bagthorpes, if they were in a good mood, quite enjoyed the Tin Shaking, but Mrs Fosdyke never did. She nearly gave in her notice over it.

'It's not good enough,' she told her cronies in the Fiddler's Arms, 'when I've done a beautiful sponge for a trifle, and one of them goes and opens a Condensed Oxtail. You could weep. And the best of it, for a grown man to have done it. If it'd been that Daisy, I could've understood it. He's mad, no doubt about it. Really mad.'

On being reminded that she had only the other evening informed them that Mr Bagthorpe was in one of his sane spells, she replied curtly that as often as not these only lasted five minutes, and now he was right back to normal—mad.

Mr Bagthorpe was certainly mad on this present occasion when his Competition Mania was revealed under Uncle Parker's irritatingly amused gaze.

'I wish you the best of luck, Henry,' he said. 'You deserve a break.'

'I shan't need luck!' snapped Mr Bagthorpe. 'Luckily for me, I don't need luck, because I never get any. All my competitions will be won by skill.'

'Will you be taking it up full time?' enquired Uncle Parker. 'You've obviously got your work cut out for a long time ahead, judging by the state of the pantry. Giving up the scripts, are you?'

'I might,' returned Mr Bagthorpe, 'when the money starts flooding in. On the other hand, it won't make any difference how many yachts and Rolls Royces I get. I'm a driven man.'

'Oh, you are,' agreed Uncle Parker. 'Though I'm surprised to hear you admit it.'

'I mean driven by my genius!' Mr Bagthorpe was beginning to shout. 'You wouldn't know about that.'

'No, I don't,' confessed Uncle Parker. 'I don't think I am a genius. If I am, I should be surprised.'

'You? *You?*' Mr Bagthorpe's voice was on a rising scale now. He stopped and looked about and suddenly noticed that he had an audience. All other Bagthorpes within earshot (and that meant a considerable radius) were now in the kitchen to find out what was going on. When they did find out, it was hideously embarrassing for Mr Bagthorpe.

'Crikey, father,' said William, after an inspection of the pantry, 'you don't do things by halves, do you?'

The larder really did look ridiculous with all its bare tins, and packets with squares cut out of them. Rosie giggled.

'You are funny,' she told Mr Bagthorpe. 'I'm going to take a photo of it for my records. Will you stand in the pantry while I take it, holding up some scissors? Really big scissors would be best, like pinking shears.'

'I most certainly will not,' he told her.

'It would be really unusual,' she said. 'It might even win a Photo Competition.'

'The day you win a Photo Competition,' Mr Bagthorpe told her, 'will be the day pigs fly.'

He was going to be proved quite wrong about this, and Rosie herself was almost certain of it, and giggled the more at the memory of the pictures of Zero, which were now away being developed.

'If you can't stop that, leave the room,' he told her tersely.

'That's rather unfair, Henry,' said Mrs Bagthorpe. 'I really think that if anyone should leave the room, it is you.'

'Right!' He seized the cue gratefully and flung off and they heard the study door bang.

'Poor Henry,' said Uncle Parker. 'It's to be hoped he wins something.'

'I'm going to,' Tess told him. 'I've sent off three already and I'll win them all. I shall win a home hair-drying kit (not that I want one)—that's a dead cert, because they're giving a hundred of them away—a fully fitted kitchen (not that I need one of those, either), and a thousand pounds.'

'Lovely, darling!' cried Mrs Bagthorpe. 'How clever you are.'

'You *think* you will,' said William jealously. 'You want to watch out. *I'm* in for the thousand pounds, as well.'

'And me,' piped up Rosie. 'But I'm not telling the others because it's a secret.'

'What about you, dear?' Mrs Bagthorpe turned to Jack.

He shrugged.

'Me and Zero don't go in for Competitions,' he said. 'They're a waste of time.'

'They'd certainly be a waste of a postage stamp in your case,' William told him.

'No one ever wins them, anyway,' Jack said.

'I did,' Uncle Parker reminded him.

'Just a fluke,' Jack said. 'I mean, I don't mean to be rude, but—'

Uncle Parker held up his hand.

'Say no more. I take your point. You are absolutely right, of course. None the less, Celia and I shall be floating about the Caribbean this time next week.'

'Oh, of course—and about Daisy,' put in Mrs Bagthorpe. 'Of course we'll have her. We'd love to.'

'I'll look after her,' said Rosie. 'I can hardly wait. Will it be all right if I put her hair in pigtails some days? I promise I won't every day, because I know it makes your hair go kinky, and spoils it, but can I *some* days?'

'You can do anything you like with it,' said Uncle Parker generously.

'Oh, thank you!' Rosie was ecstatic. 'I think she'll look even sweeter with her hair in pigtails and more naughty. I think she'll look lovely.'

Uncle Parker could have put in a word here on the subject of Daisy's naughtiness—something to the effect that if pigtails were going to make her go further in that direction than at present, they had best be avoided. He did not do this. Nobody but the Bagthorpes would take Daisy while the

Parkers were away. Nobody else would even contemplate it, with or without the knowledge that she had gone into a new Phase of Reconciling the Disparate. If he told the Bagthorpes this, even they might put their feet down. So he said nothing, and left the Bagthorpes to find out for themselves.

Chapter 5

Jack felt lonely and left out now that the Competition Entering was well under way. He did not believe that the rest of the family would win every single thing they entered, as they themselves did, but he did believe they would win quite a lot of them. Every one of them but himself was more or less a genius, and it stood to reason that only if they came up against other genii would they have any difficulty.

The Bagthorpes spent a lot of time holed up in their rooms even in the normal course of things, because of having so many Strings to their Bows. They practised instruments and read French novels and held radio conversations with names like Carlotta from Madrid or Anonymous from Grimsby. They painted portraits and wrote poetry and made calculations and did judo. Now that they were in the grip of this new mania, however, it seemed to Jack as if the only time they ever came out of their rooms was to feed. Even at mealtimes the conversation was restrained and wary. Everybody was afraid of giving something away. They didn't even make jokes any more, in case somebody else had found a Joke Competition to go in for.

Jack knew it was hopeless for him to compete with the other Bagthorpes. He had tried to write a Slogan, because he didn't like to give up too easily. He had tried putting in the right order eight reasons why he would like an electric lawn-mower (which he would, actually, because he nearly always got the job of mowing). Then he had to supply a Slogan. He thought of 'Don't let the grass grow under your feet, buy a C—— Mower tomorrow.' But he knew it was too long. He had heard Tess telling William that slogans had to be succinct. Jack went and looked this up in the dictionary and realized at once that his slogan was nowhere near succinct.

Another complication arose. It turned out that to enter a lot of these Competitions you had to sign and say you were over sixteen years of age, and in some cases eighteen. (Occasionally, of course, you had to sign and say you were *under* these ages, but the prizes for this kind of Competition were seldom very exciting.) Even

William, who was just sixteen, sometimes had to get his entries sent off by an adult. Nobody chose to have their entries sent in under Mr Bagthorpe's name because nobody trusted him to hand over any prizes that might result.

The young Bagthorpes, being of a suspicious cast of mind, even got their mother, when she obligingly sent off in her name, to sign a statement, saying:

I, LAURA FAY BAGTHORPE, HEREBY UNDERTAKE THAT SHOULD ANY PRIZE RESULT FROM MY SENDING OFF AN ENTRY FOR A COMPETITION SPONSORED BY............................... [Here a space was left for the name of the sponsor to be filled in], I WILL IMMEDIATELY PASS IT OVER TO MY SON/DAUGHTER, JACK/WILLIAM/ TESS/ROSIE (DELETE AS NECESSARY) WHO IS THE RIGHTFUL WINNER.
SIGNED: ....
WITNESSED: ....

William said he doubted if this document would hold up in a court of law, but Mrs Bagthorpe was after all their mother, and he thought they could trust her better than anyone else.

Jack trusted Mrs Fosdyke, too, but none of the others did. Jack actually got Mrs Fosdyke to send two entries off for him secretly. He preferred using her because she thought his entries were good, and might win, whereas Mrs Bagthorpe was unlikely to think this. He did not think it himself, and sent nothing else out. He really could not afford the stamps.

Jack was depressed, too, at the thought of Uncle Parker being away for a whole fortnight. He was the only real ally Jack had, apart from Zero.

'We'll have to stick together, old chap,' he told him.

As it happened, it was not Jack and Zero who were to be the butt of the rest of the Bagthorpes during the ensuing fortnight, but the luckless Daisy who was, after all, only four and not entirely accountable for her actions.

The first thing Daisy did after the departure of her parents in a flurry of gravel, was not to burst into tears as might have been expected. Mrs Bagthorpe had, indeed, been fully prepared for this, and had bought a new toy for Daisy to console her. Daisy waved till her parents were out of sight and then, with the utmost self-possession, turned and went back into the house. Rosie herself, disappointed that Daisy had not cried, because she had looked forward to cuddling her, made to follow. Mrs Bagthorpe stopped her.

'I should leave her alone a while, dear,' she said wisely. 'I expect she'll go and have a little cry by herself somewhere, and then feel a lot better.'

What Daisy was in fact doing was probably as therapeutic to her as a good cry. She was in the sitting-room where Grandpa was dozing, writing her thoughts on the walls. She did a lot of this at home and was in fact encouraged to do it by Aunt Celia, who said she herself used to do it as a child and got slapped for it by Grandma. Aunt Celia, on the other hand, was liberally-minded and believed in Self Expression. The walls of the Parker residence were accordingly thick with Daisy's thoughts and slogans. Mrs Bagthorpe had requested that she should discontinue this practice during her two weeks' stay at Unicorn House. Aunt Celia had promised she would have a word with Daisy about it.

'Though it is a pity,' she had added. 'The child needs an outlet.'

Aunt Celia might have told Daisy, or she might have forgotten, but in either case Daisy was at present finding the first of what were going to be many more outlets. She used a different colour for each different thought, and evidently considered these thoughts worthy of immortality, or at least some measure of permanence, because she used indelible felt tips to inscribe them. On her return, Aunt Celia said that she could tell in what order Daisy had written her thoughts by the way they became successively more complex and profound.

First, then, according to Aunt Celia, she wrote NO PARKING in red by the china cabinet, and proceeded to state I AM A GENIUS AND ALLWAYS RIGT in purple just by the television set. This infuriated Mr Bagthorpe, who said he could not concentrate on watching his scripts. He said Daisy's statement was always with him, right in the corner of his eye. In the end Mrs Bagthorpe fetched an oil painting of some shaggy Highland cattle out of the loft and hung it over Daisy's thought. He reluctantly admitted that this was better, but not much.

In green, by the bookshelves, occurred the more mystifying declaration A DAISY IS WITE AND YELLOW BUT NOT ME I HOP. This, Aunt Celia later explained, was part of a natural identity crisis that took place in children of Daisy's age. To this Mr Bagthorpe curtly replied that if Daisy was in two minds as to whether she was a flower or a human being (and he personally had his doubts about either), he recommended psychiatry—as he had been doing for years. Daisy was, he said, a psychiatrist's dream, and her casebook would probably make history and get published all over the world.

Daisy next drew in cobalt blue what she maintained was a donkey, but could easily have been any animal that had five sticks for legs and no ears. Under it she wrote FAR AND AWAY I WISH DO KNOK AND ENTER. She had evidently lost her original train of thought halfway, and this was agreed to be the most obscure of her motifs, particularly taken in conjunction with the drawing. Even Jack sometimes found himself looking at it and wondering what it meant.

The last and, in Aunt Celia's judgement, most interesting thought, was in livid orange, and was simply ALL THE BEES ARE DED. Aunt Celia hugged and kissed Daisy when she read this.

'I shall never ask her what it means,' she told them all. 'It is a thought that lies too deep for words.'

When Mr Bagthorpe saw Daisy's preliminary decorations of the sitting-room his thoughts were evidently too deep for words as well, because it was some time before he got anything coherent out. Mrs Bagthorpe tried to soothe him by saying that she had intended to have the sitting-room as well as the burnt-out dining-room decorated before Christmas.

'No real damage has been done,' she said, to which Mr Bagthorpe replied that considerable damage would be done to Uncle Parker's pocket, because the entire bill would be presented to him.

Most of the Bagthorpes had now collected to look at Daisy's handiwork, and they all set up arguing what would be a fair proportion to charge Uncle Parker, taking into account how many years it had been since last the sitting-room had been decorated, and how much longer it could reasonably have been expected to last. William and Rosie both started doing complicated mental arithmetic, and Jack loudly maintained that Uncle Parker was innocent anyway, because he didn't like Daisy writing her thoughts on walls, either. Jack thought Aunt Celia should pay the bill.

Had Rosie not been so eager to demonstrate her mathematical powers, she might have noticed that in the general confusion her charge had disappeared.

The murals in the sitting-room had, it seemed,

been only in the nature of an introduction to a series of similar ones all over the house. Daisy, with the battle raging below her, must have gone up the stairs backwards on her bottom, sitting on each and writing a thought or drawing or diagram at each stage of her ascent. Aunt Celia later said that these were symbolic and progressive, but nobody else could see it.

Mrs Bagthorpe found Daisy working her way along the landing, and gently persuaded her to go into Rosie's room, where she was to sleep.

'You can play with any of the toys, dear,' she told her, 'and I hope you will be very happy with us.'

She then went down to warn her husband about the stairs and landing, and sent Rosie up to keep an eye on Daisy.

'Don't let her out of your sight,' Mr Bagthorpe told her. 'We've only got Russell's word for it that she's stopped lighting fires.'

When Daisy next emerged she had her hair in little pigtails tied with large bows of pink ribbon. Rosie showed her round the family.

'Doesn't she look sweet?' she asked everybody, but no one could agree with any enthusiasm. It was already clear that Daisy, with or without pigtails, was dynamite.

What rendered the situation even more explosive was an amazing volte-face, later in the day, on the part of Grandma. She had been up in her room brooding while the row over Daisy's murals had been going on, and did not see them until teatime.

Of her three children, Henry had always been Grandma's favourite, though she would not have admitted this even under torture. Claud, her other son, was a very gentle man who took after Grandpa and hated arguments. Aunt Celia took after neither. She was, as Mr Bagthorpe and Uncle Parker both agreed (though in a very different spirit in each case), something on her own. She had then gone and unaccountably married Uncle Parker, who had committed the unforgivable crime of running over Thomas in his own drive.

Grandma had tended to lump Daisy in with her mother and father, and had never taken much notice of her as an individual. Grandma was not a very grandmotherly sort of person and had never spoiled her grandchildren as she should have done. She had never cooed over anybody in her life (unless, perhaps, it had been the cantankerous and undeserving Thomas).

When Grandma came down the rest of the

Bagthorpes were already at table in the kitchen. They were not talking about the defacement of the walls, on Mrs Bagthorpe's express instructions.

'Just don't refer to it,' she told them. 'She may not do it any more. And she is our guest, and only four, and must on no account be upset.'

She had told this to the fuming Mrs Fosdyke too.

'There's no joy in doing this house any more,' Mrs Fosdyke told her. 'What's the use of me sweeping and dusting and polishing and cooking, and the dining-room burnt to cinders and horrible scribbles everywhere you look and millions of tins you don't know what are?'

'By Christmas the whole place will be like new,' Mrs Bagthorpe promised her. In this she was right. By the end of Daisy's stay practically the whole house needed redecorating.

'And at Christmas there'll be a party, and crackers, and the whole thing'll start over again,' said Mrs Fosdyke fatalistically.

'History,' Mrs Bagthorpe told her inaccurately, 'never repeats itself, Mrs Fosdyke.'

'If it did,' she replied, 'I should have to consider giving my notice.'

While the Bagthorpes were having tea Mrs

Fosdyke was relieving her pent-up emotions by making a considerable rattle. Her temper had not improved when Tess, whose turn it was to Shake Tins, had been asked for salmon and had produced a jam sponge pudding that Mrs Fosdyke kept by for an emergency should she not be able to make her own.

'*That'll* go nice with the cucumber in the sandwiches,' she had told Tess witheringly.

The Bagthorpes were now eating cucumber sandwiches to be followed by cold jam sponge pudding. Mrs Fosdyke had declined to heat it up and make custard. There was not nearly enough to go round, and of course no question of opening another, because by the law of averages as many as fifty tins would probably have to be opened before finding such a pudding.

Grandma immediately scented excitement, and perked up accordingly.

'Is something wrong?' she enquired through a mouthful of her first sandwich. 'Have I missed something?'

'No, dear,' replied Mrs Bagthorpe, 'nothing at all is wrong.'

Mrs Fosdyke upped her clatter by several decibels and Grandma accurately received the signal. She looked round the table for clues and her eye lit on Daisy.

'Who is that?' she demanded.

'It's *Daisy*, Grandma,' cried Rosie delightedly. 'You see—you didn't even recognize her—I knew she'd look even sweeter with pigtails!'

'Hmmm.' Grandma was non-committal. She looked at her son. 'You look bad-tempered, Henry,' she told him. 'Are you in a bad temper?'

'You should know by now that I am seldom given the opportunity to be anything else,' he returned.

Grandma moved her gaze thoughtfully back to Daisy. She was putting two and two together.

'What has she done?' she asked point blank.

'Nothing,' said the Bagthorpes in unison.

'We aren't allowed to talk about it,' said Mr Bagthorpe. 'We are to pretend that nothing at all has happened. Are you, by any chance, going blind?'

'Why?' Grandma was startled by the enquiry.

'You came down along the landing,' he told her, 'and down the stairs, and you ask what has happened.'

Daisy then piped up.

'Come with me, Grandma Bag,' she said. 'I'll

show you what I did. I did some really nice things. It's just like home now.'

Mr Bagthorpe winced but held his peace.

'Finish your tea first, dear,' Mrs Bagthorpe told Daisy.

'I have finished, thank you, Auntie Bag,' replied Daisy primly. 'Sank you very much it was very nice of you to have me. Come on, Gramma.'

Grandma got up and followed Daisy from the room while the other Bagthorpes made various facial contortions at one another. Daisy and Grandma were gone a long time, and in the end Mrs Bagthorpe instructed Mrs Fosdyke to put some food aside for Grandma, and told the others they could leave the table. As a man they made for the door. They all went into the sitting-room together. Daisy turned.

'Look!' she said happily. 'Look what Grandma Bag's doing!'

What Grandma was doing was writing her thoughts on the wall with felt tips borrowed, presumably, from Daisy, as she was not known to possess any of her own.

'Oh my God!' exclaimed Mr Bagthorpe. 'I don't believe it!'

'What's she written?' William pushed his way past the others.

What Grandma had written was:

Like as the waves make to the pebbled shore
So do our moments hasten to their ends.

This was one of her favourite sayings when in one of her dark moods, and she had made a fair stab at drawing an orange skull underneath it.

She looked up. They stood together, she and Daisy, staring back at the rest of the Bagthorpes, looking suddenly and uncannily alike. There was not a hint of guilt about either of them—if anything, they each wore a look of unusual and unsullied innocence.

'I like doing that,' announced Grandma at last.

She and Daisy exchanged looks. That moment marked the beginning of what was to become known, in course of time, and not without just cause, as The Unholy Alliance.

Chapter 6

Grandma turned out to be the only Bagthorpe who got any real pleasure out of Daisy's visit. She had, the moment she took the trouble to notice her properly, at once recognized her as a kindred spirit.

'Daisy is a true Bagthorpe,' she told the others. 'She reminds me of my own grandmother.'

'Which one?' enquired Mr Bagthorpe. 'The one who ran off with the Welsh grocer, or the one that went mad?'

'She did not go mad,' returned Grandma coldly. 'She was merely eccentric. As I hope I am myself.'

'Oh, you're that all right,' he told her. 'And getting more so by the day. Dangerously more so.'

Grandma, having once crossed the frontier of doing the unthinkable, i.e. writing a thought in felt tip on the sitting-room wall, was unstoppable. She wrote her thoughts in the spaces left by Daisy. Some of her thoughts were lines from Methodist hymns inaccurately remembered from childhood, such as:

> From trials unexempted
> Thy dearest children are
> So let us lot be tempted
> Above what we can bear.

Others were short and telling:

> Henry is an insufferable show off

and:

> Age is wisdom.

She was pleased with this last, which she thought placed her in an invincible position in the household, since only Grandpa was older than she, and he did not wish to run things anyway.

Mr Bagthorpe, when he came across this, struck it out and wrote *BILGE* at the side of it, so Grandma went and wrote it in several other places and in the end he gave up and let it stand. He was incensed by Grandma's new hobby, not only because he was afraid she might start writing on walls in other places when she went out, but also because it fogged the issue of what percentage of the redecorating costs Uncle Parker would have to pay.

Once Daisy had got the place looking more like home, she lost interest in writing on walls and cast round for another outlet. Poor Rosie could do nothing at all with her. Daisy would only let her plait her hair in return for a sweet, and demanded a whole bar of chocolate in return for allowing Rosie the privilege of pushing her about the garden in an old pushchair. She refused to be sung nursery rhymes to, turned down all suggestions of a Teddy Bear's Picnic in the meadow, and put her hands over her ears if Rosie tried to read her a fairy tale. She declined, in short, to be sweet and cuddly and adoring, and the devoted Rosie was sorely tried, though she never, as a Bagthorpe, gave up.

On the fourth day of her stay, Daisy left Grandma happily writing thoughts on the landing walls, and set off in search of something Disparate to Reconcile. It was very unlucky that on this partic-ular day Mr Bagthorpe had gone out into the garden and omitted to lock his study door behind him. (He had taken to doing this since Daisy first arrived. He said that he did not want her thoughts on his walls, and furthermore he felt her vibra-tions alone would be sufficient to stop his creativity dead in its tracks for weeks, if not months.)

Daisy had a full hour in the study and was very

happy and occupied during this time. When she came out she even allowed Rosie to take her by the hand into the garden and push her on the swing. They softly sang together, and Mrs Bagthorpe, who was cutting flowers for an arrangement, looked fondly at them from a distance and thought what an idyllic picture they made.

Idylls, however, are made to be shattered, and Mr Bagthorpe shattered this one very rudely. On his return to his study he realized at once his oversight and hardly dared look at his desk. When he did, his worst fears were realized. He had left lying on his desk his latest script, typed in rough, and beside it the loose pages of the original manuscript. Both were missing. Also on the desk had been a buff envelope, stamped but not yet addressed, in which Mr Bagthorpe had intended to send off his typed draft.

No one but Daisy knew the details of what had happened during that happy and creative hour spent in the study, but repeated cross-examinations did produce some kind of picture.

Daisy, it appeared, had never seen loose typewritten pages before, and what Mr Bagthorpe's typescript had looked like to her, had been pages missing out of books. As two of the study walls were lined with shelves it had seemed reasonable to Daisy to assume that on them were the books with the missing pages. She discovered, however, that Mr Bagthorpe's paper was too large for most of the books, and had found a pair of scissors, and adjusted this discrepancy, though being careful in each case not to cut off the number at the top of the pages because she would need this when she started fitting them into books. Mr Bagthorpe's carpet was accordingly littered with long strips of paper with one or two words typed on each.

Once she had the pages cut to size, Daisy set about the arduous task of inserting them into various books from the shelves. She chose these books quite at random, sometimes because she liked the cover, sometimes because she liked the title. She soon discovered that none of these books had pages missing as she had expected, but this she soon remedied by simply tearing them out anyway. Mr Bagthorpe's waste bin was filled with shredded pages from books, each numbered from one to eighty, but each from a different book.

Daisy had then turned her attention to the manu-script itself. This, being handwritten, had looked to her like a very long, untidily written letter. She had therefore placed it in the buff envelope. She did not fail to note that it had not been addressed, and knew that it should be, so she made up what sounded an interesting name and address, and wrote it in large capitals. She looked about her, could see nothing else urgently in need of attention, and went off in search of someone to post the letter. It so happened that Mrs Fosdyke was about to go to the village for groceries, and she stuffed the envelope into her bag with ill grace, and went off.

When this later emerged, Mr Bagthorpe put her in the same category as Daisy, and stated that he considered her equally to blame.

'Where in the name of heaven did you think that accursed infant got a stamp for thirty pence from?' he demanded.

'I did not look at the stamp, Mr Bagthorpe,' replied Mrs Fosdyke stonily. 'It has never been part of my duties to look at stamps.'

'What was the address, then, for crying out loud?' he yelled.

'Don't shout, Henry dear,' interposed his wife.

'I don't look at addresses, neither,' returned Mrs Fosdyke virtuously.

'Was it England, for God's sake?' shouted Mr Bagthorpe. 'Was it Leeds, Brighton, Rome, Timbuctoo, Japan—'

'It's no use your asking,' she interrupted. 'I never even looked.'

Mr Bagthorpe tore out, got into his car, and drove in more or less Uncle Parker's style to the village to see if he could catch the letter before it went. He was too late. Ten minutes later he was back, dragging his feet.

'Gone,' he said. 'An original manuscript. Irreplaceable.'

'It is a terrible thing to have happened,' agreed Mrs Bagthorpe sympathetically. 'Have a cup of tea.'

'And to crown all,' he continued, '*this* had just arrived.'

He flung down a brightly coloured postcard with an exotic stamp. It was from Uncle Parker, somewhere in the Caribbean.

'Lovely!' cried Mrs Bagthorpe, snatching it up. She read aloud:

'"Celia and I are in Paradise. We wish you were here, especially Henry. There are enough ideas on this cruise to keep him going for a year. Has he won a yacht yet? We like Paradise so much we may even stay on longer at our own expense." Oh, isn't that lovely!'

'Lovely?' shouted Mr Bagthorpe. 'If he's staying

96

on out there, that delinquent daughter of his can be sent after him.'

'Why are you shouting, Henry?' asked Grandma, entering at this juncture. She looked calmer and happier since she had taken to writing her thoughts on walls than she had ever done during her Breathing Period.

'Tell her, Laura.' Mr Bagthorpe threw himself into a chair and buried his head in his hands.

'The child is a true Bagthorpe,' said Grandma when she had heard the story. 'There is not another child on earth whose mind would have worked like that.'

'Amen to that,' said Mr Bagthorpe grimly. 'And what about my script? I refuse to commit suicide, though I am tempted to.'

'Eventually, Henry,' his wife told him sensibly, 'your script will be returned to you with NOT KNOWN on the envelope. It may take a day or two, or even longer, but it will be sent back. You must be patient.'

'Sent back, will it?' said Mr Bagthorpe. 'The Royal Mail maintain a resident clairvoyant, do they?'

'What do you mean?'

'I mean,' he replied, 'that I am not in the habit

of writing my name and address at the top of every script I write. I write the title, Laura, as is usual in such cases.'

'Oh. No. Of course.' Mrs Bagthorpe was temporarily floored. 'Never mind,' she said, 'we can turn it into a game.'

'Laura,' said her husband, 'you are wandering. I am talking about the irreplaceable loss of a priceless piece of creative work, and you are talking about a game. We are at cross purposes.'

'We are talking about exactly the same thing,' she said firmly. 'We shall all go to the study after tea and we shall play Hunt the Script.'

Mr Bagthorpe vetoed this instantly and emphatically. None the less, in the privacy of his study, he was himself to play Hunt the Script during the next few days. This involved taking down almost every volume in the room (there were library steps in there, and Daisy had dodged from shelf to shelf) and first of all retrieving all eighty of the cut-down pages. He had then collected nearly two hundred strips of paper, and armed with Sellotape set about attaching them to their counterpart pages. None of this did he regard as a game. He found it tedious, tiring and, at times, hopeless. Eventually, however, he fitted the jigsaw together and set about retyping the rough draft, this time in duplicate.

So traumatic an effect did this incident have upon Mr Bagthorpe that for the rest of his life he compulsively typed everything in duplicate, and kept all his duplicates in a locked chest. From time to time he would type (in duplicate) bills to Uncle Parker for all the extra paper involved, but these were never paid. All sane people, Uncle Parker declared, typed things in duplicate, and he maintained that Daisy had done Mr Bagthorpe an invaluable service in bringing this point so strongly home to him.

Before setting about playing Hunt the Script, Mr Bagthorpe telephoned the travel agency to find out Uncle Parker's whereabouts in the Caribbean. He then sent an expensive cable to the effect that if Uncle Parker did not return on the appointed date, Daisy would be put on the next ship to the Caribbean in care of the stewardess.

'So far as I am concerned,' he said, 'the lot of them can go round the world in circles for ever, like the *Flying Dutchman*, or whoever it was.'

Grandma, the minute she found out what he had done, sent a cable saying, 'Daisy is a true Bagthorpe and can stop here for ever.'

She was crafty enough not to tell anyone about this. And neither she nor Mr Bagthorpe knew that Mrs Bagthorpe privately sent her own cable, saying, 'Ignore storm in tea cup.'

Later during Daisy's stay there was to be another spate of cables. The response to these first three was a semi-hysterical call from Aunt Celia on a very crackly line. She refused to speak to anyone but Daisy, and when Daisy got on the line nobody could tell from her end of the conversation what was being said at the other end.

The Bagthorpes gathered round unashamedly to listen, but gleaned nothing. Daisy was saying things like, 'I like Grandma Bag', and 'I helped Uncle Bag with his scips', and 'We had peas an' custard for dinner again today.'

When she put the receiver down she turned to the others and said, 'Mummy was crying, I think. I wish she was here, so's I could make her feel better.'

Mr Bagthorpe said nothing, but his expression spoke volumes.

'Goodness alone knows,' Grandma said, 'how Celia ever managed to produce such a jewel of a child.'

The others looked at her sharply. It began to

appear that Daisy was in line to succeed Thomas in Grandma's affections. If so, it boded ill.

The two of them went off together and Rosie looked forlornly after them. The only time she ever had Daisy to herself was at night. When she went up she would tuck Daisy in unnecessarily, and look fondly down at her and arrange teddy bears and rabbits around her. (This was for Rosie's own gratification—Daisy awake would have no truck with soft toys.)

'Never mind, dear,' said Mrs Bagthorpe, seeing her daughter's downcast face. 'Go and practise your violin. Henry, what *are* you doing?'

Mr Bagthorpe was writing on the wall.

'These are my walls,' he said, 'and I am writing on them.'

He was writing:

Hell is other people and their children

Chapter 7

During the second week of Daisy's visit it seemed at first that an unaccustomed lull fell over the Bagthorpe household. The Competition Entering was falling off as they ran out of Competitions to enter and, in the case of the younger Bagthorpes, funds.

'It's an investment,' William told his mother, when she timidly suggested that perhaps he was over-spending on magazines and stamps, and buying commodities he was never likely to use, simply in order to enclose part of their packaging with his entry.

'What, for instance,' she asked him, 'will you do with three giant tubes of suntan cream? They will hardly make suitable Christmas gifts.'

'At Christmas,' he replied, 'I shall be skiing in Austria, or else in Tenerife. I shall need a lot of suntan cream. I shall ask Atlanta if she wants to come with me.'

Mrs Bagthorpe looked very dubious at this (it reminded her of her Problems) but said nothing.

Daisy seemed to have gone into a Quiet Phase. She had not written anything on the walls for a week, though other people had. If the walls were to be redecorated anyway, no one wanted to miss the chance of writing something clever on them. As small children they had never been allowed to do this, and must have been harbouring secret ambitions in this direction, judging by the spate of thoughts and bons mots that streamed from them.

Even Jack did it. He tried to get Zero into most of the things he wrote, not because he thought Zero could read them and be encouraged by them, but because he hoped they would have an effect on the family.

He wrote, for instance:

Zero is a dark horse

and

Zero could do anything he wanted to, he just doesn't want to.

He also wrote zero hour is coming under which William wrote prepare to meet thy doom under which Mr Bagthorpe wrote if the day of *judgement is coming I hope to god at last we'll see some justice done* underneath which Grandma wrote *Amen.* Grandma usually had the last word.

Daisy's Quiet Phase lasted until the Tuesday of the second week.

'She has really settled down beautifully,' Mrs Bagthorpe said, 'and it's delightful to see how happy she and mother are together.'

'I don't agree,' returned her husband. 'That pair are as dangerous as—' here he stopped for want of a strong enough simile, and gave up. 'They're terrorists,' he said. 'They'd stop at nothing.'

Grandma, as it happened, had very little to do with the events of the second Tuesday, though Mr Bagthorpe did not believe this, and always maintained that she had put Daisy up to them. Grandma did not contest this because she wanted to feel she had played a part in them, and really wished that she had.

It was in fact Mr Bagthorpe who unwittingly triggered the whole thing off by a chance remark at lunch. He was talking about Uncle Parker, because another card had just arrived, even more irritating than the first.

'It *would* seem like paradise to him, of course,'

said Mr Bagthorpe. 'Because he's never done a day's work in his life. Lying around swigging gin and doing crosswords—in his element, of course.'

'What's an element, Uncle Bag?' piped up Daisy, whose mother had told her always to ask the meanings of words she did not understand.

'You tell her,' Mr Bagthorpe told William.

He did not care to enter into conversation with Daisy, because it interfered with his pretence that she did not exist. He used this kind of 'blotting out' technique with Zero, as well, and was always pretending he had never set eyes on him before. Jack, in a bold moment, had once challenged him directly about this.

'If I thought that mutton-headed hound was going to stop here for ever,' Mr Bagthorpe had replied, 'I should lose my sanity. It's a necessary defence mechanism.'

Tess and William both started to explain to Daisy what an element was, the former using a literary approach, the latter a scientific. Tess was talking a lot about Shakespeare and Chaucer, and not only told Daisy what an element was, but what a humour was as well. On the whole Daisy listened more to Tess than to William, and the latter gave up in the end, saying:

'We outgrew Chaucer and that lot centuries ago.'

Afterwards he said he was glad Tess had told Daisy what an element was because it was a responsibility he wouldn't wish to have to live with.

The rest of the meal Daisy went very quiet and thoughtful, but nobody noticed this. The Bagthorpes rarely noticed other people.

Daisy, being after all only four, had grasped only dimly what an element was. Tess had, however, mentioned fire and water in the same breath, and this had struck a chord. Later, Aunt Celia was to claim that it had struck an ancient, primitive, unconscious chord, and showed at how deep a level Daisy's mind was already working. Mr Bagthorpe then said that the word he would use was not deep, but low, and a semantic argument had developed out of this that drew the fire off Daisy altogether. This may even have been what Aunt Celia intended. She was certainly very expert at defending Daisy and had probably had to develop this art, being her mother.

Fire and water, then, became inextricably linked in Daisy's mind. She already knew about fire, of course, and probably felt she had experimented far enough with this element for the time being. Water, however, was something else again. Daisy had done hardly any experimenting with water other than splashing about in the bath and paddling. A whole new world seemed to open up for her. She must have spent the rest of the meal silently thinking about water, and what she would create with it. Even so, it was a relatively short time in which to develop an all-out obsession, which was what Daisy appears to have done. All the Bagthorpes got obsessions but nobody had ever developed one quite so quickly as this before.

Daisy's behaviour during that afternoon was that of an all-out obsessive. It was as if, had she had the necessary tap to hand, she would have flooded the whole world. It later turned out that 'Noah's Ark' was one of her favourite stories, and she also had a record of 'Captain Noah and His Floating Zoo' which she never tired of hearing. She probably really did believe that if she turned all the taps on and waited, the Bagthorpes would be going two by two before the day was out. This prospect, to the four-year-old mind, was understandably attractive, though in the event there were only two other people who said they could understand it—Aunt Celia and Grandma.

Things would not have developed to the pitch they did, however, had not Mr and Mrs Bagthorpe decided to go into Aysham that afternoon to see a French film. William, Tess, and Rosie accompanied them, but Jack said that he did not like French films.

'The subtitles have gone before you have time to read them properly,' he said.

Tess scornfully told him that when you went to a French film you were supposed to be listening to what was being said, not reading English. Jack openly admitted that his French was not up to this, and said that he intended to take Zero for a long walk. Daisy, then, had been left in the charge of Grandma and Grandpa, neither of whom appeared to have any qualms about the matter.

Mr and Mrs Bagthorpe set off leaving Grandpa having his post-prandial doze, Grandma and Daisy playing Ludo (in which, astonishingly, Grandma allowed her partner to win occasionally), and Jack setting off across the meadow with Zero.

Jack had said that he was taking Zero for a walk, which was true, but not the whole truth. It was becoming increasingly clear that Zero had a potential that until recently had never been allowed to develop. Now that he could Fetch, and Beg, Jack intended to add another skill to his repertoire.

That'll make *three* Strings to his Bow, Jack thought with satisfaction.

What Jack had in mind, was that Zero should learn to find his way back home from a long distance. This he had never been able to do. If he ever wandered out of calling range, what he always did was to sit or lie down, and wait till he was reported missing and a search party sent out. This party usually consisted of Jack alone, though sometimes Rosie came too, on the off-chance that something exciting might have happened that she could keep a record of.

Once Zero had mastered this, Jack intended to give him a period of intensive training so that he could develop into something between a homing pigeon and a bloodhound.

He had given a lot of thought to the method he would adopt to bring about this end. To some extent he would have to be ruthless. Zero had to be genuinely lost. This meant that Jack, when Zero was looking the other way, would have to swing into a tree or else dodge away behind a hedge, leaving Zero absolutely on his own.

There was no reason to suppose that Zero would not then adopt his usual tactic of slumping down and waiting to be found. Some other element had to be added to the situation to make it possible for Zero to extend himself. This was where the bloodhound aspect of the operation came in.

For a week now, Jack had been stuffing his washing—T-shirts, socks, underwear and so on—into a duffle bag instead of the laundry basket. He had got this idea, indirectly, from a dimly remembered telling of 'Hansel and Gretel'. Instead of dropping pebbles, Jack was going to drop clothing. If Zero sniffed around enough he should, with the aid of these clues, gradually work his way home.

He'd follow my scent to the ends of the earth, Jack thought fondly. He's a one-man dog.

None the less, he realized that Zero was going to have a shock when he found himself thus heartlessly abandoned—much more than Hansel, who had at least overheard his stepmother planning the whole thing, and had prepared for it. Accordingly, Jack spent the outward journey throwing a lot of sticks for Zero, and doing a great deal of patting and praising. He hoped that this would help Zero not to take the necessary desertion too personally.

Halfway across the meadow Jack opened the duffle bag. Everything in there seemed suitably smelly and would give Zero a good strong scent to follow. He waved a sock under Zero's nose.

'Sniff, boy!' he commanded.

Zero sniffed obligingly and growled and made to worry the sock. Jack snatched it away and threw a stick. While Zero was fetching it Jack surreptitiously let the sock drop, and walked on. He kept this kind of thing up for the next mile or more. At intervals of around two hundred yards he dropped an item of clothing. He ran out of clothing to drop in the middle of a spinney.

It seemed an ideal place to set about losing Zero because he was very much preoccupied by rabbits and squirrels. He had never yet caught a rabbit (indeed Mr Bagthorpe swore to having once seen Zero pursued across the meadow *by* a rabbit). Nor, of course, had he ever caught a squirrel, though it was not for want of trying. He ran round trees barking at them and making great futile bounds, and gave the impression that he thought if he practised these often enough he would get to be able to fly, and corner the squirrels that way.

Jack watched him now, and felt at heart a traitor. He could not even say goodbye. It would be cheating.

'It's all for your own good, old boy,' he told him silently. Zero was in full pursuit now, prancing into the distance after a squirrel running above. Jack saw his chance. He turned and ran. He did not stop until he was right out of the spinney. Very faintly he could hear Zero still barking.

Jack looked about for the vest he had dropped at the edge of the spinney, but could see no sign of it. There was not much wind and so it could not have blown away.

It doesn't matter if I can't see it, he thought. I can't sniff it out like Zero can. He'll do it.

He set off confidently home, walking fast in case Zero caught up. From time to time he caught a glimpse of a sock or T-shirt. The trail was still intact.

It was Jack's misfortune, then, to be the first to encounter Daisy's flood. Because he was there when the Bagthorpes returned, upstairs with Grandma, he too was counted as an accessory after the fact, and came in for a good share of Mr Bagthorpe's fury.

Jack met the flood at the kitchen door. (There were several separate floods—one, in fact, for each source of water in the house—but this happened to be the first.) He looked down at his feet.

'Crikey!'

Water was actually flowing under the door. He pushed it open. The deserted kitchen was awash. Drifting over the tiles in little mad flotillas were empty paper cake-cases in rainbow colours, which were, Daisy later explained, 'the Navy'. Jack did not at the time know this. He stood and boggled and wondered by what strange kind of accident they had come to be there. Here and there was a wooden spoon, a peg, and, like a raft, the bread board.

Jack was so thrown by this amazing sight that it was nearly a full minute before he registered that he could not only see water, he could hear it. His eyes went to the sink. Then he threshed his way through, ankle-deep, to the taps. By the sink was the chair Daisy had stood on to reach them. Still he heard water. Jack groaned. He splashed his way to the utility room. As he passed the open larder he could see a giant packet of Sugar Coated Puffballs drifting aimlessly past the vegetable rack.

When this tap was turned off there was relative quiet. Jack listened. Still he heard water, dripping now, steadily and heavily. He went back into the kitchen and raised his eyes. Water was seeping in droplets, gathering, and splashing down on to the flood below.

In the hall the parquet was just covered and the rugs squelched slightly—as did his shoes. He pushed open the door of the sitting-room and saw water coming down the walls and through the ceiling.

Grandpa sat dozing, as yet high and dry. Jack decided to leave him. There was no immediate threat to his life, and it would take more time than Jack could afford to explain to him what was happening—even had he known.

Instead he ran up the stairs two at a time, to meet a fresh flood on the landing. Now he could hear Daisy's voice.

'Soup, soup, bootiful soup,
Booootiful pea green soup!'

Horrified by the implications of this chant, Jack threshed his way to the bathroom. His worst fears were confirmed. Daisy had poured a whole bottle of green bubble bath into the overrunning bath and washbasin. She said afterwards that this was to make things more real, that she wanted the water to look like the sea, all green and foamy. When Aunt Celia heard this, she murmured something about 'the foam of perilous seas in faery lands forlorn', and clasped Daisy to her.

'She is going to be a poet,' she told everybody.

Daisy at present wore only her knickers and was busy ladling the green water out of the bath and into a flower bowl.

'Hello, Zack!' she squealed, seeing him. 'It's lovely—oooh, it's lovely!'

114

He rushed past her and turned off all the taps.

'This is soup, Zack,' Daisy told him, apparently not noticing that the supply had been arrested. 'Bootiful pea green soup. It's not cold enough for sea, so it's soup.'

Jack looked helplessly about him. He did not know where to start.

'And upstairs,' continued Daisy happily, 'there's a fountain and waterfall.'

Jack rushed for the door and bounded up the next flight of stairs. The shower, trained directly at the floor, was at full pressure. Jack put one arm across his face to shield it, and advanced. He was soaked from head to foot by the time he had groped for and found the taps. A telltale chair, its padded velvet saturated, stood by the basin.

Jack really did not know what to do. He stood mesmerized and noticed that he had little green bubbles fringing the bottom of his trousers. Should he dial 999, he wondered? Did the fire brigade deal with floods as well as fires? He decided probably not. He went down and found Daisy just about to enter Grandma's room.

'I'm taking Grandma some soup,' she told him. Jack actually found himself opening the door for her. Grandma was sitting by the window, a book in her lap, asleep.

'Wake up, Grandma Bag!' shouted Daisy. 'It's dinner-time!'

Grandma blinked her eyes and snorted and turned.

'What? What's that?'

'Look!'

Daisy triumphantly plonked the flower bowl on the dressing-table, and green water and foam slopped out.

'Soup, Grandma Bag,' Daisy told her. 'I know it's foamy, but it's not sea, I promise. It's too hot for the sea.'

'Thank you, Daisy,' said Grandma, recovering herself and realizing she was caught up in some kind of game.

'You haven't got a spoon.' Daisy trotted to the door. 'I'll fetch you one. I bet the ocean's full in the kitchen.'

'A true Bagthorpe,' Grandma told Jack as she disappeared. 'What *is* the child talking about?'

'Grandma . . .' Jack croaked. 'Grandma . . .'

He had to be careful, he realized. Grandma was seventy-five. He had to break it to her gently. He was still working out the best way to do this when

116

from down below came blood-freezing yells of fury and despair. The rest of the Bagthorpes had returned. It turned out that Mr Bagthorpe had looked in the previous week's paper by mistake, and the French film was not showing. He hated to be wrong, but he hated above all to be seen to be wrong, and had driven back to Unicorn House in a mood of suppressed fury.

When he opened the kitchen door this fury instantly became unsuppressed. He had waded across the kitchen and was now standing, wet to his knees, in his study, and yelling:

'Through a locked door! I don't believe it! Through a locked door!'

Jack left Grandma and ran halfway down the stairs. Through the open study door he could see his father's soaked trousers and shoes, and hear dripping and spattering. Mr Bagthorpe's desk had been flooded.

The rest of the day was, even by Bagthorpe standards, memorable. Their annals were not without incident, but this particular event still stood out even years later.

Daisy's flood divided the camp. Grandma and Rosie both fell heavily on to Daisy's side, Jack was neutral, his mother tried to be, and the rest were ranked against her. A fresh batch of cables was sent off at enormous expense, as Mr Bagthorpe was to discover when his telephone bill arrived.

Mr Bagthorpe's own cable was to the effect that if Uncle Parker did not return immediately and remove his unhinged daughter, he, Mr Bagthorpe, would not be responsible for his actions. It also advised Uncle Parker to hang on to his money, as he would need every penny he possessed to restore the Bagthorpes' ruined house and furniture.

Grandma's cable said: DAISY IS A TRUE BAG-THORPE STOP SHE CAN STOP HERE FOR EVER STOP SHE IS A SHINING JEWEL OF A CHILD, and Mrs Bagthorpe's: IGNORE HENRY BUT DAISY REALLY HAS BEEN MOST TRYING.

The Bagthorpes had certainly been tried, as in Grandma's inaccurately quoted Methodist hymn (for 'so' read 'but', and for 'lot' read 'not').

> *From trials unexempted*
> *Thy dearest children are*
> *So let us lot be tempted*
> *Above what we can bear.*

Chapter 8

Some measure of the dimensions of the Bagthorpes' latest disaster can be deduced from the fact that the very elements, it seemed, came out in sympathy. It was like something out of Shakespeare. The witches on the blasted heath, the storm on the eve of Caesar's death, the tempest in *The Tempest*, all reflected the turmoil going on in human lives. And to the benighted Bagthorpes, the gale that blew up out of nowhere around teatime seemed like a direct expression of their own agony.

The Bagthorpes knew it was teatime only by the clock. There was no question of anybody actually having any tea. The devastation was hideous. Even as Mrs Bagthorpe summoned her resources and tried to think what Stella Bright would do under similar circumstances, the sky began to darken and the first eddies of the gale rattled the windows.

'Go and look at all the beds,' Mrs Bagthorpe eventually told Tess, 'and see how many of them are wet. That is first priority, I think. The rest of us will all remove our footwear, because being barefoot will not be nearly as dangerous as having damp shoes or socks.'

The rest numbly and obediently took off their footwear with the exception of Mr Bagthorpe, who made a point of ignoring any sensible suggestion his wife might make.

'It'll be quicker to tell you whose beds are dry,' said Tess, returning. 'Grandma and Grandpa's, and Jack's. Everybody else's is wet.'

Mrs Bagthorpe had a sudden inspiration. It was Mrs Fosdyke's half day but she was well known to love calamities that happened to other people. This was one of her truly human traits.

'Jack,' said his mother, 'take your bicycle and go and ask Mrs Fosdyke whether she could kindly come and help us.'

'You stop where you are,' Mr Bagthorpe told him. 'We've enough troubles already.'

'Don't be silly, dear,' his wife said. 'Mrs Fosdyke's help will be invaluable.'

'Why not invite a whole team of harpies while you're at it?' enquired Mr Bagthorpe. 'What about that pair that sit either side of her in the Fiddler's Arms? They'd enjoy it.'

'What a sensible idea!' exclaimed Mrs Bagthorpe.

'Jack, please ask Mrs Fosdyke whether Mrs Bates and Mrs Pye could come along too? Really, we can't have too many helpers.'

'Who we really want is Hercules,' said Mr Bagthorpe. 'He is the one person I can think of who's had any kind of training for this kind of job. Why can't we be an ordinary, happy family like everybody else? All I want is to be happy. Tomorrow I may go and see Aunt Lucy in Torquay.'

His wife pursed her lips. He was waiting, she knew, for her to point out that he detested visiting Aunt Lucy in Torquay. (He did so because she had few surviving relations, and was rich.) This would then give him the cue to say that he did, indeed, detest doing this, and did so only when driven. Mrs Bagthorpe usually fed her husband with cues fairly readily, but at the present moment was in no mood for it.

'Hurry up, Jack,' she contented herself with saying. 'And tell Mrs Fosdyke that if she is able to come Mr Bagthorpe will collect her in his car— and her friends as well, of course.'

'Why will I?' he demanded. 'She moves fast enough.'

'Because it is the polite thing to do,' Mrs

Bagthorpe replied firmly. 'Especially as she will be doing us a favour, and it is such a stormy night.'

It was then that Jack remembered Zero.

'I can't!' he cried. 'I've got to go and look for Zero!'

'I don't suppose he's drowned,' said Mr Bagthorpe. 'That would be hoping for too much.'

'He's not here—he's out!'

'If you are going on your bicycle he won't be going with you,' said Mrs Bagthorpe. 'It's dark now, and it would be most dangerous. Do hurry, dear.'

Jack did not care now how much he went down in the estimation of the family. All he could think of was Zero, lying in the darkened spinney, the wind and rain buffeting about him and his eye fixed dolefully ahead for a sign of a rescuer.

'You don't understand!' he said desperately. 'Zero's lost. I left him up in that spinney the other side of The Knoll.'

'Jack, do *hurry*,' repeated Mrs Bagthorpe, urgently wringing out her cloth. Jack looked helplessly about him. Everyone was either wringing out a cloth or wielding a ladle or saucepan. Concern for Zero was at an all-time low, he could see that.

He rushed out. The wind was so strong that he could hardly steer a straight course. The rain lashed against his face and he had a picture of Zero, sodden now, his fur flattened, still lying there, waiting.

Mrs Fosdyke was just sitting down to a cup of tea when Jack hammered on the door.

'What's all the banging for, then?' she demanded. 'I'm not deaf, you know. You better come on in— look at you—drenched to the skin. Does your ma know you're out?'

'She sent me.' Jack explained about the flood, but felt that words could not really do justice to the awfulness of it.

'Everything's sopping,' he ended. 'Absolutely sopping.'

Mrs Fosdyke had sat sipping her tea as he said his piece. Now she set her cup down.

'There's plenty,' she observed, 'that'd give their notice over this.'

'Oh, there are,' Jack agreed. 'And I wouldn't blame them.'

'I don't suppose it's worth asking if that child has had her backside tanned,' she continued.

'Will you come?' Jack was impatient to be gone. 'And will the others?'

'I can't speak for them, of course,' replied Mrs Fosdyke with maddening prevarication. 'They might, or they might not.'

Mrs Fosdyke knew full well that unless they were prevented by an Act of God, they would not only come, but do so with alacrity. They were inveterate inspectors of the interiors of other people's houses. By now they had seen the inside of most houses in the village by various means, varying from the legitimate—attending a coffee morning, perhaps—to the more devious methods of delivering unnecessary messages or selling raffle tickets.

The Bagthorpe residence had, however, proved an impossible nut to crack. Mr Bagthorpe had told his wife that any coffee morning would be held over his dead body. If anyone came round collecting money for any cause whatsoever, he would either slam the door in their faces, or start shouting and go on shouting after the luckless collector right down the drive.

Mrs Bates and Mrs Pye, of course, often plied Mrs Fosdyke with questions in the Fiddler's Arms, and by now had a fair idea of the geography of the place, and knew that the television set was hired, and that the best dinner service was Royal Worcester and that there was a chair in the hall that had been sat in by William the Conqueror. (This last being a drastic piece of misreporting by

Mrs Fosdyke, who did not always quite follow Mr Bagthorpe when he was being sarcastic.)

'I don't know if I *want* them to come, for that matter,' said Mrs Fosdyke now.

'Why on earth not?' Jack felt he must have understated the case badly. 'Honestly, the whole house is sopping—it'll take half the night to clear it up.'

'Because,' replied Mrs Fosdyke, none the less rising and donning her coat, 'I have my pride.'

Jack was mystified by this declaration, but relieved to see that Mrs Fosdyke evidently was going to ask them.

Mrs Fosdyke was, indeed, torn between soliciting the help of her two cronies and dissuading them from giving it. She had secretly cherished the hope that one day they *would* see the interior of the Bagthorpe residence, but on a day when she had everything polished to the last degree of brilliance, the silver set out on the sideboard and the artistic flower arrangements trailing everywhere.

From what Jack had said it was clear that the look of the place, far from being at its best, was probably at an all-time worst. On the other hand, she often described to Mrs Pye and Mrs Bates how she suffered in the service of the Bagthorpes.

Sometimes she had the feeling that they did not quite believe her, that they had no real grasp of the kind of people the Bagthorpes were. She felt powerless to put it adequately into words. The nearest she had come was once after the recent tin-opening ceremonies.

'Sometimes,' she had told them over her third Guinness, 'it comes over me that when I get up that drive I've left the whole world behind me. And when they all got hooting over that asparagus I'd meant for a trifle I could've took to my heels for ever. It was like one of them mad Dracula films on Friday telly.'

Now, then, was clearly the moment when her friends should witness the Bagthorpe life as actually lived, even if it was not the optimum time from the aesthetic angle.

'I'll ask 'em,' she said, whipping her chiffon head-scarf into a tight knot. 'But I can't promise. You wait here.'

Three minutes later she was back, her face glistening wet and unnaturally excited-looking.

'They'll come,' she announced. 'And a storm you've never seen the like of. Thunder and lightning and the lord knows.'

'I heard it,' Jack said. 'I saw it. I'll go to the

phone box and let father know. He'll pick you up in the car.'

Mr Bagthorpe was less than enchanted to hear that Mrs Fosdyke and Co. were coming to mop up. He did not know Mrs Pye and Mrs Bates, but this had not prevented his having formed an unshakeable opinion of them. From time to time he popped into the Fiddler's Arms himself for a quick snorter and the three of them were invariably present, their eyes like gimlets above their glasses of stout.

'All they want is a guillotine behind them, and some knitting,' he said, 'and you'd have it to the life. They are waiting, I swear, for severed heads to roll. They are the Three Furies. They're Valkyries. They're termagants.' Mr Bagthorpe never minded mixing his metaphors in the interests of piling on an effect.

'In the name,' came his voice over the crackling line, 'of all that is wonderful, I want to know why this kind of thing keeps happening to me. Why can't we be happy like other families?'

'I've told them you'll pick them up,' Jack told him. 'And tell mother not to worry if I'm a bit late. I've got to go and get Zero.'

'Hell's,' came Mr Bagthorpe's gritted voice, 'bells!' and the line went dead.

The storm seemed right overhead now. Jack flinched and ducked each time the lightning tore down. He hated storms. He usually spent them in his room, the curtains drawn, under the bed with Zero. Zero hated storms as well. His ears went right down and he shook all over and seemed to shrink nearer the ground. Now he was crouched all alone in the spinney.

And thinking I'm a traitor, thought Jack. This was the worst part. He had deliberately abandoned Zero. It was with the best of intentions, but Zero could not be expected to know this.

I feel like Judas Carrot, Jack thought.

He banged on Mrs Fosdyke's door again.

'I'm leaving my bike in your porch!' he shouted above a clap of thunder. 'I'm going over the fields.'

He began to run to forestall argument. Sure enough he heard her voice following him.

'Here! You don't go near trees, you hear? You'll be strucken. Come back! What'll your ma-a-a say?'

Jack turned his face manfully away from the village and went out beyond the lights into the utter darkness of the meadow. The storm racketed about him and lit the scene every minute or two with a weird brilliance. The worst moment, the one that stood out ever after, was when something clammy and white slapped over his face from out of nowhere, blinding him. Jack yelled and stumbled and clawed at the empty cloth. He held it out at arm's length and the lightning flared. It was one of his own aertex vests.

Jack groaned. He had forgotten the carefully laid trail of laundry in his concern for Zero. Even now, his priorities seemed clear. All hell, it was true, would break loose later when the loss of his underwear and socks were discovered. Hope that they would ever turn up, in whatever condition, was slight.

But they're dead anyway, Jack thought as he panted on, the vest stuffed in his pocket. Socks and pants can't suffer the way Zero can. He'd die for me, I know he would. So it's up to me to die for him.

He reached the spinney at last and drew a deep breath. Mrs Fosdyke, he knew, had been right about trees. They *did* attract lightning.

But at least we'd go together, he thought. He climbed the fence and pushed his way through the brambles towards the clearing, and began to call now, above the din of the wind and thunder.

'Zero! Zero! Come on, boy, it's me. Zero!'

He stopped dead. He was in the clearing. A long

flare of lightning lit the whole scene distinctly. Jack shut his eyes and opened them again.

'Zero!' he called, forlornly now. Again the lightning flared. The clearing was deserted. Zero had gone.

By the time Jack returned an hour later Mrs Fosdyke and Co. were in occupation and had taken over the whole operation. To the dazed and stricken Jack it seemed for a few moments when he pushed open the door that he was seeing treble. He saw three Mrs Fosdykes wringing, darting, pouncing, and heard three of them clucking. It was an extension of his nightmare and he actually groaned aloud.

Mrs Bagthorpe came in then, and obviously her yoga and breathing had failed her in her extremity, because she became almost hysterical at the sight of her son, drenched, mud-spattered, white-faced and staring.

'I did tell him.' Mrs Fosdyke paused and leaned on her mop. 'And if he'd been struck dead it'd've been no wonder.'

'I wouldn't care if I had been,' said Jack dully.

Mrs Bagthorpe advanced to put her hand on his head but he pushed it away.

'You might be delirious!' she cried. 'You sound as if you are raving!'

He went blindly among the mops and bucket brigade and into the hall.

'Take off your wet shoes,' called his mother help-lessly after him.

Jack trudged up the stairs past Daisy's mottoes and along the landing and into his room. He stood and stared disbelievingly. He actually knocked his forehead with a clenched fist to settle his brains, as Mr Bagthorpe sometimes did. Then a wet Zero was prancing at his knee, tail going as it had never gone before, and giving little excited snorts.

'O Zero, Zero, good old chap!' Jack had to sit suddenly on the bed and Zero danced about his feet.

He's safe, thought Jack. And he found his way home. Even without the trail he did it. He's a genius!

It later transpired that Zero had arrived back only moments after Mr Bagthorpe had replaced the receiver after his conversation with Jack. He had squelched through the kitchen, slipping and cursing under his breath, opened the back door, and been bowled to the ground by Zero in full tilt. His front paws, aimed at the middle of the door, had landed flat on Mr Bagthorpe's chest. He had leapt clean over him, straight past a squealing Rosie and Tess who were mopping, up the stairs and into Jack's room.

'Like a rat,' Mr Bagthorpe afterwards said, 'into its bolt-hole.'

He asserted that not even during active service in a war had he been so rudely and unexpectedly assaulted.

'Even war has rules,' he said. 'There's an International Code. That hound knows no bounds. This family is going to have to split up. People are going to have to make a choice between the hand that feeds them and the teeth that bite it.'

When Jack pointed out that Zero had never in fact bitten Mr Bagthorpe, he dismissed this as a quibble.

'How I ever rose again is a mystery,' he declared.

How Zero actually got home was a mystery, even Jack admitted this. He had certainly not followed the trail. In the end, Jack decided that Zero had been quite capable of finding his way home all along, but had just never felt like it before.

'He just needed a good *reason* to do it,' he explained to the others. 'Like a storm, for instance.'

They remained unconvinced. Zero never repeated the performance, so perhaps they were right. But then, never again did Zero find himself alone at night in a spinney with a storm raging about him. The question was left open.

Chapter 9

The clearing of the Bagthorpes' house after Daisy's Flood lasted approximately till Christmas. It was a complicated operation—the walls needed doing on two separate counts, and other parts of the house too had been subjected to both Fire and Flood. In any event, for the next two months or so the house was never at any given moment free of workmen of one kind or another. They were not called in, however, until the preliminary mopping up had been completed by Mrs Fosdyke and her brigade, who took an unconscionably long time over this and were, Mr Bagthorpe asserted, actively enjoying it.

'They are in their element,' he declared. 'They feed on destruction and human misery. Only a corpse discovered in some dark corner could make them happier.'

There were days on which he said he might well be driven to supplying one or two such corpses himself.

He detested Mrs Pye and Mrs Bates even more heartily than he did Mrs Fosdyke, and perhaps the only good thing that came out of the matter for him was that from this time on he did not see Mrs Fosdyke as the ultimate in aggravating and purblind humanity. He had seen worse, his eyes had been opened. He particularly detested Mrs Pye who, he maintained, was upsetting the vibrations of the whole house to the point where he could hardly bring himself to write a single word.

When asked to describe what it was in particular about Mrs Pye that had this effect, he was at a loss to put it into words that convinced anyone else of her direfulness.

'Haven't you noticed the way she holds her mop?' he would demand. 'And have you ever seen anyone scrub the way she does? She scrubs like she was Lady Macbeth outing a damn spot.'

Mrs Bagthorpe dismissed all these allegations as farfetched and fanciful, though she herself had been irritated by having descriptions of her house relayed to the interested village, and then repeated to herself by acquaintances. Their home had been represented, she said, as a large-scale hovel.

'It *is* a hovel,' returned Mr Bagthorpe flatly. 'It

135

became a hovel within an hour of that accursed infant being left here.'

He absolutely ignored Daisy for the remainder of her stay, and was itching for Uncle Parker to return so that he could tell him what he thought of her, and have the biggest all-out row he had ever conducted with him. He had the advantage, he knew, of having all the ammunition, and also several days in which to compose choice insults and exquisitely worded sneers. He went about the house tripping over brooms and pails, rehearsing these, and also made notes of them while in his study. Jack caught snatches of them, and trembled for Uncle Parker.

At the same time he could not help feeling a certain thankfulness that somebody had done more to invoke his father's anger than himself. Mr Bagthorpe had certainly taken the loss of the laundry relatively lightly. Beyond remarking that if only Zero had been struck by a thunderbolt the socks of the entire household would have been well lost, he had little to say.

It was Mrs Fosdyke's wrath that had been particularly incurred. First she dispatched Jack and a protesting Rosie on a full-scale search of the fields along the route Jack had taken. Jack took Zero

136

too, though not with any real hope of his sniffing out the missing articles.

'You can't expect him to,' he told Rosie, as they plodded disconsolately through the long, sodden grass. 'Even a trained bloodhound couldn't do it after all that rain.'

'You *know* Zero can't sniff things out,' she told him crossly. 'He never has been able to. Father says he couldn't even sniff a mutton bone at five yards.'

They returned, predictably, empty-handed, and with Zero's ears at a pronounced downward slant. He must have understood some of the things Rosie had been saying. Jack took Zero up to the sanctuary of his room before going down to tell Mrs Fosdyke that the search had been fruitless.

She had cast pregnant looks at Mesdames Pye and Bates, who rolled up their eyes and clucked in sympathy.

'You see now,' she told them, not without a certain satisfaction, 'what I'm up against. You see now what I have to cope with.'

They nodded sagely. They did, they said.

'That washing,' Mrs Fosdyke declared, 'must've been worth all of ten pound. Twenty, I shouldn't wonder, and all want replacing. Your ma'll have to be told.'

Mrs Bagthorpe was accordingly told, but she had other Problems to occupy her mind. Not only did she have to oversee the restoration of Unicorn House, but now she was worried about Daisy.

'She is psychologically disturbed,' she told her husband. 'It is a definite sign.'

'Psychologically disturbed?' he repeated on a rapidly ascending scale. 'Is this supposed to be news? Are we supposed to leap to our feet and cry Eureka? Psychologically disturbed, she says!'

What had happened was that Daisy had begun to hold lengthy conversations with somebody called Arry Awk. It was Rosie who first noticed this. She hovered around Daisy a good deal, partly in the hopes of a chance to plait her hair or push her on the swing, and partly because she was afraid that if she committed any further misdemeanours Mr Bagthorpe really would despatch her somewhere on a boat.

On the morning after the deluge Daisy had, for the first time, voluntarily returned to Rosie's room straight after breakfast. Rosie, hopeful that this meant that she wanted, at last, to play, followed after her. She could hear Daisy's voice as she went along the landing.

'You are a bad boy, Arry Awk,' she was saying.

Then, 'You are my bestest friend in the whole world, Arry Awk.'

(At first the Bagthorpes had not known quite what to make of the name of Daisy's invisible friend—and, it later transpired, accomplice. It was some time before they realized that she had read the name on a framed and illustrated version of 'Widdecombe Fair' that hung in the downstairs lavatory along with Spanish bullfight posters and Victorian texts.)

When asked who Arry Awk was, Daisy replied that he was the person who had turned on all the taps in the house on the previous day. It was this that worried Mrs Bagthorpe.

'It is a clear case of transference,' she said. 'Whatever shall we do?'

Her husband replied that the main thing to do was make sure that Arry Awk turned no taps and lit no fires for the next three days, and that thereafter he would be the sole concern of Uncle Parker and Aunt Celia.

'And Uncle Tom Cobley and all, as far as I am concerned,' he concluded. 'The whole pack of 'em—Dan Stewer, Bill Skewer, Peter Gravy—you name 'em.'

'You are being silly, Henry,' said his wife. 'This

is a serious matter. Daisy is only four years of age and is a guest and under our protection. She is holding conversations with an invisible friend called Arry Awk, and we must think what to do about it.'

'You think,' he told her. 'I'm through with thinking. But if you really want to know what I think, it's that this Arry Awk who has suddenly cropped up is part of a malicious and well-laid plot.'

'Whatever do you mean?' cried his wife.

'I mean,' he returned, 'that we are coming to the nub of the whole thing—the Insurance, and the compensation. If that crazy infant makes out she's crazy, and that it wasn't her that went writing all over everywhere and reducing this house to a shanty—if she makes out it was this Arry Awk fellow that did it, where are we then with the Insurance?'

'Surely we are adequately insured?' queried his wife.

'We are adequately covered by any normal standards,' he replied. 'I had imagined we were insured against every possible contingency—I extended the cover, you remember, after mother's Birthday Party. But we are *not* insured against the total devastation of the entire house by an invisible entity by the name of Arry Awk. There is not an Inspector in England who would entertain such a claim. You could scrutinize the small print until you were cobalt blue in the face and find no possible loophole through which you could conceivably slip this Mr Awk.'

'All right, dear,' replied Mrs Bagthorpe. 'I perfectly understand. There is no need to labour the point.'

'Some points *need* labouring,' returned Mr Bagthorpe, 'and this is one of them. I do not wish to hear any more about the matter. And just keep her out of my way. I am an easy-going man, but I must not be tried beyond endurance.'

The next trial of Mr Bagthorpe's endurance was to take place the following day, with the arrival of the first prize resulting from the recent spate of Competition Entering. This prize was not for Mr Bagthorpe. It was not even for anyone whom he could have *borne* to have won. It was, incredibly, for Grandma and Daisy.

No one had any inkling that Grandma had been entering competitions, let alone Daisy, and the Bagthorpes erupted in a manner that was highly gratifying to Mrs Fosdyke, who felt that now, at last, her friends would understand what it meant to move even on the fringes of their lives.

'I can certainly see,' conceded Mrs Pye, above Mr Bagthorpe's yelling and William's thundering tattoo, 'that you have your hups and downs, Glad.'

'It's always like this,' she told them. 'I've tried to tell you, and now you can see for yourselves.'

'I wouldn't have your job,' agreed Mrs Bates, 'for all the tea in China, and shudder to think how near I come to getting it.' (She had been an unsuccessful applicant for Mrs Fosdyke's position years before.)

To win this prize Grandma had, of course, cheated. Mr Bagthorpe felt particularly hamstrung about this. He longed to expose her, but knew that in so doing he would bring humiliation and ridicule on the whole family including, inexorably, himself. He was forced to accept the thing, if not stoically, at least relatively silently, when other people were about.

The way Grandma had cheated was in representing herself to be a regular user of a particular brand of toilet soap. This falsehood had been extended to cover Daisy's ablutions, too. Mr Bagthorpe contended that Daisy was not in the habit of using any soap whatsoever, so far as he was aware, let alone Blue Lagoon Lanolin Enriched, and it was well known that Grandma would consider nothing but Pears. She had once gone four days without washing when the village shop was temporarily out of stock.

Mrs Bagthorpe, although a very conscientious person, did not take this aspect so seriously.

'A bar of Blue Lagoon Lanolin Enriched was purchased,' she said, 'and mother and Daisy obviously gave glowing accounts of its performance. And Daisy has the skin of a peach, and will look perfectly lovely in the advertisements.'

'If that child has the skin of a peach,' he returned, 'then we have yet another demonstration of cosmic chaos and injustice. She deserves to have the skin of a blackcurrant. She has not, to my knowledge, washed since she has been here. We must now hope that she has not contrived to win a prize for a toothpaste slogan.'

Some men from Blue Lagoon Lanolin Enriched soap came swiftly on the heels of the letter to confirm the good tidings, and in fact Mrs Bagthorpe did have time to bundle a protesting Daisy into the bath before she was presented.

'Arry Awk never has bafs,' she squeaked. 'Arry Awk 'ates bafs!'

'It is not Arry Awk who is to be photographed for an advertisement,' Mrs Bagthorpe reminded her, adding cunningly, 'nor who is to win a thousand pounds.'

'When I get my money,' Daisy confided in a voice muffled by a soapy flannel, 'I shall buy a pussy. If I have enough money, I shall buy two.'

'You will have enough money for a *thousand* pussies,' Mrs Bagthorpe rashly assured her, thereby laying the foundations for a months' long battle of wills between Daisy and her parents.

It transpired that what the Blue Lagoon Lanolin Enriched Soap Company had been in search of, was a family who had used their product through the generations (this despite the fact that it had been on the market only a few years). What they wished to do was photograph both Daisy and Grandma (the latter suitably touched up to look half her age) and use it in conjunction with a Slogan to the effect that if one used Blue Lagoon Lanolin Enriched Soap regularly, one could confidently expect to have much the same skin at seventy as one had at four.

Grandma herself was delighted by the idea, and told endless fibs to the Blue Lagoon men. One of them was about her age, from which she subtracted five years. When she later saw the touched-up portrait of herself, she regretted, she said, that she had not made it twenty.

These men were particularly interested to meet Daisy. They had not expected, they said, to be lucky enough to find a child so young for their advertisement, as most children of that age were not able to read, let alone write. Grandma thereupon proudly took them on a conducted tour of Daisy's slogans, by which they seemed suitably impressed, if bewildered. One of them asked, rather hesitantly, whether perhaps there had been a recent accident? He made vague gestures towards the surrounding signs of Fire and Flood.

'Not an accident,' Grandma told them loftily, 'but yet another manifestation of my granddaughter's creative genius. She is a shining jewel of a child.'

At this, Mr Bagthorpe, who had sat back grimly swallowing every one of Grandma's pronouncements so far, showed signs of imminent cardiac collapse and left the room suddenly.

Daisy herself then appeared, well scrubbed and happy at the prospect of a thousand kittens in the offing. Obligingly she went through her paces for the benefit of the Blue Lagoon men, who were

145

clearly staggered at having lighted upon so uncommon a ménage. They had been prepared for the unusual after reading Daisy's testimony on behalf of Blue Lagoon Lanolin Enriched soap—it had read 'I was my face in blue lagon sope and I wash my hands and my toes and my tumy and all over and I am a genius and allways rite'—but were none the less bowled over by meeting its perpetrator.

Daisy confessed early on that she did not in fact use Blue Lagoon soap.

'I don't wash very much,' she told them. 'Auntie Bag made me just now and I did 'cos of the fousand pussies but Arry Awk never does.'

The pair of them nodded bewilderedly at this cryptic confidence, but at the same time begged her to let it be a secret among themselves.

'If anyone ever asks you,' they pleaded, 'just *pretend* you use Blue Lagoon soap, will you? You know, like a kind of game.'

'Tell a fib, you mean?' asked Daisy disconcertingly.

'I could not for a moment countenance that,' said Grandma at once. 'That child is a miracle of innocence and truth.'

'Of course, of course,' the Blue Lagoon men agreed hastily, 'and we wouldn't *dream*—'

'And it was no part of the Competition,' went on Grandma piously, 'that anyone was to tell any untruths.'

'Of course—'

'We are not *paid* to tell untruths,' she continued, 'or to act parts, or call it what you will. We will receive one thousand pounds each prize money, with no strings attached. I shall probably buy a fox fur with my money, and some ecru underwear.'

'I wouldn't mind *'tending* to wash,' piped up Daisy who seemed, uncannily, to have caught Grandma's drift. 'Would I get paid extra?'

There was a silence. No one could take exception to such a suggestion coming so artlessly from one so young. It seemed, indeed, to have a simple and childlike logic.

'If I did,' went on Daisy speculatively, 'I could get even *more* pussies.'

'I am certain that something could be arranged,' said the senior Blue Lagoon spokesman, avoiding his colleague's eye.

'Neither Daisy nor myself,' put in Grandma swiftly, thus including herself in the deal, 'will find it easy to tell untruths—or rather, pretend.'

'Of course not,' said the Blue Lagoon man, by now thoroughly mesmerized.

'So if you will draw up a contract,' went on Grandma smoothly, 'we shall be able to sign it when your photographer comes.'

Soon after, the Blue Lagoon men took their leave in a daze, while the Unholy Alliance exchanged happy glances. Mr Bagthorpe, when he heard of the extra payments to be made to Daisy and Grandma, went into a fresh series of apoplexies.

'Machiavelli,' he ended by declaring, 'was a beginner. Lucretia Borgia was a novice.'

It seemed to him that the only thing in life he had to look forward to now, was the return of Aunt Celia and Uncle Parker.

Chapter 10

The confrontation that took place on the return of the tanned and pleasantly smiling Parkers was, indeed, something of a landmark in Bagthorpian rows. What marked it out, apart from the four-, five-, or even at times six-cornered nature of the battle, was the presence of a kind of Greek Chorus of assorted workmen, all of whom, at some stage, downed tools to listen and even, from time to time, participate. There was no doubt that this gave the whole thing an extra dimension, and added to its already epic quality.

Sorting out the various claims and counter-claims, weighing the comparative rights and wrongs of the different parties, would have presented a gargantuan problem even to a trained legal mind. The threads of debate were so intricately ravelled that the workmen could not be expected to follow them, and were accordingly always weighing it on the wrong side.

They made the natural mistake, to begin with,

of assuming that Grandma and Daisy, in view of their respective extreme age and youth, were automatically innocent. Because Aunt Celia was so beautiful, and did so much weeping and clasping of her only child to her bosom, they tended to exonerate her, too. When Uncle Parker affably offered each workman a duty-free packet of cigarettes, there was really very little doubt in their minds as to who was the real villain of the piece, especially as he did so much yelling.

They had been influenced, too, by Mrs Fosdyke (who missed the row owing to an urgent appointment with the dentist). She had kept them liberally supplied with hot beverages, on condition that they should drink these out of sight of Mr Bagthorpe. He was, she told them, so mean-minded that he would as likely as not begin hurling these hot drinks about and even scald somebody. They were inclined to believe this.

Jack, who had an untypically Bagthorpian sense of fair play, thus found himself, for the first time he could remember, actually in sympathy with his father. He became particularly irritated by Aunt Celia's moans and warblings and claspings of a reluctant, and even struggling Daisy. Along with his parents, he was unconvinced by the elevation of ALL THE BEES ARE DED to the status of mystic utterance. He even risked putting his own oar in.

'But all the bees *aren't* dead,' he protested during a momentary lull. Aunt Celia cast on him a look of disbelieving pity.

'Oh, so literal!' she murmured. 'Whence is it fled, the visionary gleam—and so young!'

Jack had no way of answering this remark, of which he could make neither head nor tail.

The row raged on for something near two hours. To plot its course was near impossible since at any given moment it was hard to know who exactly was ranged against whom. Grandma changed sides the most. The row kicked off with the writing on walls issue. Grandma came right out and said that her spell of writing on the walls had been the best days of her life since she had lost Thomas, and that she would feel everlasting gratitude to Daisy for this. She intended, she added, to alter her will.

None the less, Uncle Parker was about to concede that perhaps he had better contribute a couple of tins of paint, when Daisy gave the whole battle an unexpected turn by announcing loudly:

'I di'n't write on the walls, so there. Arry Awk did. He's a bad boy.'

'Arryawk?' echoed Aunt Celia faintly. She ran

the syllables together and the way she said the name gave it a distinctly different sound, like that of an Arab Oil Sheik or Indian Spirit Guide. She made it sound a quite different name.

When she finally understood who Arry Awk was, she became, even for Aunt Celia, decidedly distraught. Her hairpins fell out and her ringlets tumbled wildly down and the plumber and carpenter and their mates gazed fascinated.

At this point Grandma, who never minded taking two sides at once in the interests of stirring things up, proclaimed that she, too, wished Arry Awk to go away. She was tired, she said, of hearing everlastingly about Arry Awk and how bad he was.

This was, of course, a clear case of jealousy. Daisy had now become the light of Grandma's life. She saw that awful child through glasses as rose-tinted as she had ever directed on the late Thomas. It seemed to her that just as she had lost him under Uncle Parker's wheels, so she was now in danger of losing Daisy to Arry Awk.

'She talks more to that awful Arry Awk than she does to me,' she complained. 'There is no such person, and I demand that you get rid of him instantly.'

This brought such squeals of protest from Daisy herself that Grandma swiftly modified her position.

'All I meant was,' she explained, 'that I wish Arry Awk would speak up. So far, I have had difficulty in hearing him. Any friend of Daisy's is a friend of mine.'

When the row swung round to Daisy's Flood, Mr Bagthorpe did so much yelling that the carpenter and his mate set to hammering on new skirting boards. The plumbers, after a swift exchange of glances, initiated their own sabotage by fetching a lot of pipes and clanking them about. When the speech, and the Greek Chorus's racket, ended more or less simultaneously, Uncle Parker was left, in effect, with no case to answer.

All he in fact said was:

'I'm sorry you feel like that about it, Henry,' and Daisy added:

'It wasn't me. It was Arry Awk.'

To which Grandma, eager to reinstate herself, added:

'Of course it was.'

Where Mr Bagthorpe made his big tactical mistake was in leaving the matter of his desecrated script to the end. He himself felt this to be the most outrageous of Daisy's misdemeanours and had saved it as his climax. The rest, however, were left relatively cold by the matter. As his father's voice rose and fell Jack could sense that the heat had gone, the atmosphere was cooling, interest dying off. Right in the middle, Grandpa entered and nodded all round to everyone and switched on the television. The sound was off, but most of the company present, including the workmen, found their eyes wandering to the screen. Mr Bagthorpe, unaware that his sound and fury were signifying nothing, carried on.

He made a further tactical error. Throughout the row he dwelt obsessively on the subject of money. He did a lot of yelling about paying bills and whose moral responsibility they were. The result of this was that the plumber and the carpenter and their mates informed Mrs Bagthorpe at the end of the day that they wished to terminate their services. Their estimation of Mr Bagthorpe had sunk to the point where they saw that the likelihood of their bills ever being paid was slight, if not non-existent. They had accordingly decided to cut their losses and go.

They did not tell Mrs Bagthorpe this, of course. They made excuses about ailing old mothers and so forth, and Mrs Bagthorpe enquired of them how much was owed. With alacrity they fixed on a sum and she wrote out a cheque then and there. They hastily collected their tools and left. (Mr Bagthorpe was in his study making notes about the row.)

When he emerged his wife unwisely told him what had happened, and he was just beginning to shout again when the front door knocker banged. Mr Bagthorpe almost ran through the hall and flung open the door. Jack, who happened to be halfway downstairs, heard the typical, snapped-out 'Well?' and saw in the porch a colourful young man and woman, carrying briefcases and wearing a lot of shoulder-bags and cases on straps.

'Mr Bagthorpe?' he heard the young woman cry. 'Oh, congratulations! Oh, you happy, happy family!'

'Oh *what?*' repeated Mr Bagthorpe incredulously. 'Who are you? What are you selling? I don't want any.'

Slowly Jack descended. He had the feeling that he might be going to witness something interesting. The girl caught sight of him.

'And that must be Jack!' she exclaimed. 'Oh, Jack—I feel as if I know you already!'

Mr Bagthorpe and Jack were now equally nonplussed. The only way the former could think of for dealing with this enigmatic pair was to slam the door in their faces. It was not as if it were an unusual thing for him to do, even at the best of times.

From the other side came peals of merry laughter and even outright giggles.

'My God!' exclaimed Mr Bagthorpe. 'Listen to that. They're lunatics.'

'We know you and your little jokes, Mr Bagthorpe,' came a teasing girlish voice.

'My little jokes?' Mr Bagthorpe now banged a fist against his forehead—always a bad sign.

'Get out of here!' he yelled at the front door. 'Get the hell out of here!'

There were further giggles from the other side, a whispered conference, and then footsteps receded over the gravel. Mr Bagthorpe stood and listened, then shook his head dully.

'I think I have a persecution complex,' he said. 'That felt like persecution to me. Even complete strangers are after me now.'

'They knew your name,' Jack pointed out. 'And they said something about congratulations. Mind you, they did seem a bit mad.'

'I should have been a monk.' Mr Bagthorpe was soliloquizing now, walking slowly back to the kitchen where he had left his current row half finished.

'Yoooeeeh!'

He stopped in his tracks. Jack and his father gaped. The girl they had just banged the door on was now, incredibly, inside the house and poking her head round the corner at the far end of the hall.

'Your turn now!' cried the head. 'Count ten first!'

The head vanished.

'Did you see that?' Mr Bagthorpe asked after a pause.

Jack nodded.

'There is a mad female at large in my house,' said Mr Bagthorpe slowly and carefully. He was clearly trying very hard to keep a hold on his own reason. 'This female knows my name. She wishes to play hide and seek.'

'Looks like it,' Jack agreed. 'The only thing is, mother's in the kitchen. She must have let them in.'

'She—' Mr Bagthorpe strode forward and flung open the kitchen door, looking wildly about him as he did so. Jack peered past them.

'Where are they?' yelled Mr Bagthorpe. 'What d'you mean by letting 'em in?'

'Ssshhh!' hissed his wife. She put a finger to her lips and looked meaningly towards the pantry. He looked incredulously at her. In the silence that followed there came another sharp rap on the knocker that caused Mr Bagthorpe to leap into the air. Jack made a move.

'Don't answer it!' came the order. 'The whole asylum's probably out there.'

'Answer it, Jack,' said his mother firmly.

'I'll do it!' snapped Mr Bagthorpe. 'Here!'

He snatched up a small meat-axe from the rack of kitchen tools.

'Henry!' wailed his wife.

Jack followed him through into the hall. His father flung open the front door. Beyond the raised arm and hand brandishing the axe, Jack could see the telegraph boy. He recognized him because the Bagthorpes went in a lot for telegrams. The boy was cowering away, the yellow envelope clutched up against his chest.

'Give me that!' ordered Mr Bagthorpe, lowering the axe. The boy held it at arm's length and it was whipped away. Mr Bagthorpe tore open the envelope and ran his eye over what Jack could see was a very long telegram, as telegrams go. Later everyone in the family read it. It said:

CONGRATULATIONS YOU HAPPY BAGTHORPES
STOP GREETINGS TO YOU ALL MOTHER FATHER
GRANDMA GRANDPA WILLIAM ROSIE JACK AND
MOST OF ALL YOU LUCKY TESS STOP YOU ARE
OUR HAPPIEST FAMILY IN ENGLAND STOP SUE
AND JEREMY ARE ON THEIR WAY TO TELL YOU
ALL OUR MARVELLOUS PLANS FOR YOU STOP
CONGRATULATIONS AGAIN AND SINCERE
REGARDS STOP JOHN STONE CONTROLLER
BORDERLAND TELEVISION

Mr Bagthorpe was in no state to take in the
full import of this communication. The words
that really seemed to stand out in it were 'happy'
and 'lucky'. He at once pounced on these as firm
evidence that the telegram was some kind of
hoax.

'Where did you get this from?' he demanded.
'Let's see your credentials.'

'Is it . . . is there any answer?' stammered the
boy, preparing to mount his bicycle.

'Of course there isn't!' snapped Mr Bagthorpe.
'How in the name of all that's wonderful could you
reply to a burble like that?'

The telegraph boy skidded off over the gravel

and Mr Bagthorpe looked down at the telegram again. He looked at it in much the same way as an angler might look at what he had taken to be a fish but which turned out to be a part of a recently dismembered corpse.

'Oh, Henry, darling!'

They both turned. Mrs Bagthorpe, looking unusually pink, was advancing on them with a pronounced air of sweetness and light.

'Oh, darling, wait till you hear!' she cried.

'You can cut out the darling bit,' replied her husband. 'Read this.'

He thrust the telegram at her and she gave it, surprisingly, only the briefest of glances.

'It's all true! Oh, Henry—Jack—go and tell the others!'

'Tell them what?' Jack asked.

'Tell them'—she was positively girlish now—'tell them that we have been chosen as The Happiest Family in England!'

'*What?*' said Jack and his father together.

'The Happiest Family in England!' She clasped her hands together. Even Jack felt irritated.

'Laura,' pointed out Mr Bagthorpe, 'you know, and I know, that we are *not* The Happiest Family in England. You are deluded.'

'It was a Competition—Tess did it. Oh, Jack—
do fetch the others. Fetch Tess, fetch everyone!'

Jack started up the stairs.

'Even Grandma?' he enquired.

'Of course. Oh, Henry, darling, do come into
the kitchen and meet our guests. They're so thrilled
you would think it was *they* who had won.'

She took him by the arm and Mr Bagthorpe,
looking like a tiger that has been given a tran-
quillizing dart and is being led meekly into
captivity, went with her.

Jack told Grandma the news first. He had to
repeat it three times because she kept thinking she
must have misheard him.

'But we are *not* The Happiest Family in England,'
she said, using almost exactly the same words as
her son. 'Wherever did these people get that
impression?'

'It's something to do with some Competition
Tess went in for,' Jack told her.

This made more sense to Grandma, who had
cheated to win her Competition, and did not deny
others the same licence.

'I'll come down, I suppose,' she said, beginning
to rummage round for extra rings to wear, 'because
I always, as you know, put the family first. I

personally am not in the least happy, and don't feel as if I shall ever be happy again now that Daisy has gone. A light has gone out of my life.'

William had to remove his headphones to receive the news. There was a lot of crackling going on inside them and other noises that gave the irrational impression that he had contacted a duck.

'Quick,' he said. 'Get on with it. I've made a contact.'

Jack told him the news in as few words as possible.

'So what's that to do with me?' he asked. 'Tess's lookout, not mine. Happy. That's a joke.'

'I think mother wants us all to go down and look happy,' Jack told him.

'There's nobody can force me to look happy if I'm not,' William returned. 'And I'm not. Go away, will you?'

'All right,' Jack said. 'Shall I tell them you don't want the prizes, if there are any?'

He shut the door and went along to Rosie's room. She was standing at her easel with tears running down her face and dripping off.

'Cheer up, Rosie,' said Jack. He did not feel that Rosie was going to pass as happy in the immediate future.

'I'm doing a portrait of darling little Daisy,' she sniffed. 'She wouldn't let me do one while she was here. I think she was too shy. I shall hang it where I can look at it when I lie in bed.'

'That's a really good idea,' Jack told her encouragingly. 'Look . . .'

He went on to impart the news.

'B-but I'm n-n-not happy!' Rosie dropped her brush and began to sob in earnest now. Jack felt that there was a depressing sameness of reaction to the news he was imparting.

'Well anyway, Rosie,' he said, 'if you can manage to look happy even if you aren't, you might win a prize. I should wash your face before you come down.'

Tess was the only person to be made unfeignedly glad by the news. She was too glad, Jack felt. She positively smirked.

'We'll be on television!' she sang, giving her hair a swift brush. 'Won't father be *furious*? Oh, clever me!'

'I wouldn't get too excited,' Jack told her. 'Nobody's very happy at the moment. They might take the prize back when they see we're not happy. I'll go and tell Grandpa. He usually manages to look quite happy.'

Tess, he reflected as he went to fetch Zero, was going to be insufferable for a long time to come, and the worst would be brought out in the others. Mr Bagthorpe would be moody, and William at his most caustic.

None the less, within less than half an hour the entire Bagthorpe ménage was foregathered in the kitchen, which was still the most presentable room in the house. Jack himself arrived last, because he had spent some time praising Zero to try to get his ears up and create an impression of happiness.

Everyone was talking very loudly. Most people were boasting. Jack sat and listened and gradually pieced together what was happening. Borderland Television wanted to make a film about a Real Live Happy Family, and show it to the nation on Christmas Day.

'Nobody has ever done it before,' enthused the girl, who wore striped socks and whose name was Sue.

'It's an absolute breakthrough,' affirmed the long young man, who had a beard at one end and stained suede shoes at the other and whose name was Jeremy.

They stayed for a long time drinking coffee and outlining Borderland Television's schemes. (These included cash payments for all the Bagthorpes, which was fortunate because it made it easier for them to appear happy for the time being.)

Sue then produced copies of Tess's winning entry, and handed them round.

'These are a Press Release,' she told them, and Tess preened herself.

'A Tess Release,' she murmured.

No one laughed.

Jeremy then took a lot of photographs with a Polaroid and the pair finally drove off with much waving and calls of 'au revoir!'

'Well, isn't it all thrilling?' exclaimed Mrs Bagthorpe, turning back into the house. 'You really are clever, Tess dear. And won't it be fun?'

'It will drive us all,' predicted Mr Bagthorpe, 'to the brink of breakdown. If we have to look happy for more than five minutes on end, the strain will prove too much.'

'Nonsense, dear,' said his wife. 'All we have to do is to be our own natural selves.'

As it happened, she was more or less right about this. Tess's entry about her Happy Family was a masterpiece of subtlety. She had foreseen difficulties should she actually win, and had therefore cleverly admitted, for instance, such things as her father's shouting and William's sarcasm, and turned them around so as to make them appear expressions of extreme happiness and affection. Jack took his own copy of the entry up to his room and read it aloud to Zero in the hope that the spirit of the thing would get through to him.

'My family,' he read, 'is the happiest in England if not the whole world. And practically every member of the family is a genius, which makes their happiness all the more remarkable. Take my father. He is a creative writer, and also the most lovable eccentric in the world.' (Mr Bagthorpe took Tess up sharply on this, later. 'I am not lovable,' he declared. 'I have never been lovable.')

As Jack read on, he could see why Tess had won the Competition. She really had made the Bagthorpes sound happy. She had even brought in the Parkers and made *them* sound happy as well. She described Grandma's cataclysmic Birthday Party as the kind of lighthearted, careless junketing that was the very stuff of life as lived by the Bagthorpes.

Jack was impressed. He thought it weird that Tess should write the truth in such a way that it came nowhere near the actual truth. He was pleased to see that Tess had included Zero, and said how much happiness he gave to the whole family, and what hilarity Mr Bagthorpe created by insisting that he did not like him.

'D'you hear that, Zero?' Jack said. 'Father *likes* you. He really does. And Tess says—now listen to what she says about you: "At the very centre of this happy family is their pet dog, and because he is all in all to them, they have called him, with true Bagthorpian upside-down humour—Zero." Hear that, Zero? That's you. Good old boy!'

Zero took the reading calmly. Mr Bagthorpe's opinion did not seem to matter to him any more. He had, though Jack could not know this at the time, inklings of what was to come.

Chapter 11

Mrs Fosdyke was frankly disbelieving when told about the Bagthorpes' overnight promotion to The Happiest Family in England.

'I never heard such nonsense,' she said briskly to Jack, who was first down. 'Happy indeed! Whatever next!'

'And we're all going to be on telly on Christmas Day,' he went on. 'Including Zero.'

'The programmes at Christmas is always rubbish,' declared Mrs Fosdyke deflatingly. 'They're never in this world going to make a film in this house, the state it's in?'

'They are,' Jack nodded. 'They said they wanted us exactly as we are. They thought the Fire and Flood sounded really interesting and happy.'

Mrs Fosdyke snorted.

'P'raps they'd like to come to tea one day,' she said, 'and have a dish of oxtail trifle, and see how happy *that* makes 'em. Whose turn is it today? Not that it makes any difference.'

She was consulting the Tin-Shaking Rota on the pantry door.

'Mr Bagthorpe Senior. Ah well,' she drew a deep sigh. 'No better and no worse than anyone, he ain't, and at least a gentleman with it. You don't get *him* hooting at baked beans for a fruit salad. *Apologize*, he does, every time, ever so handsome.'

'Grandpa is polite,' agreed Jack.

'Where's them workmen got to?' enquired Mrs Fosdyke. 'Here by now, they ought to be. Are they coming or not? We shall never get this place straight.'

Jack told her about the row and about the workmen's decision. Mrs Fosdyke was not surprised, and said so.

'More than ordinary flesh and blood's used to, the goings on in this house. There'll be workmen giving their notices every five minutes. Bound to be.'

She was wrong about this. Later workmen, not having had the benefit of hearing Mr Bagthorpe's diatribe about bills, tended to stay on, despite all setbacks, out of sheer curiosity. They wanted to see what happened next.

Quite apart from the daily rituals of Tin Shaking,

and the average once-a-day furore, a lot of extra things began to happen to the Bagthorpes during the ensuing weeks.

The Competition Entering began to pay off, sometimes in surprising and even unwelcome ways.

Mr Bagthorpe's first win, for instance, entitled him to a free stay at Tallbuoys Health Farm. He won this by accident. It was, as his wife pointed out, his own fault for not reading the small print. The Competition had been run by the makers of a well-known fresh-orange drink, and what Mr Bagthorpe had really been after was a fortnight at a first class hotel on the island where the oranges were grown. He was disgusted by his runner's up prize and the letter that came with it, which ended up by wishing him a 'happy, healthy future with Betta Orange Juice'.

'I have read about Health Farms,' he said, 'and have no intention of entering one. I should return an attenuated wreck addicted to soya beans and raw yeast.'

'Oh really, Henry,' protested his wife, 'they are the most splendid places. You would return lithe and fit for Christmas, and have rubbed shoulders with the rich and famous.'

'I have no wish to rub shoulders with the rich and famous,' he replied, 'particularly in a Turkish bath. Like who, for instance?'

Mrs Bagthorpe reeled off a list of well-known politicians, TV personalities, and film actresses who were all known to be regular patrons of Health Farms.

'It would, of course, be useful material for future scripts,' he mused, the names of two of his own favourite film actresses having figured in Mrs Bagthorpe's list.

'Of course it would,' she agreed. 'Why not write and say that you will go the week after next, the last week in November? It will be so quiet there and it must be very hard for you to write with the house so full of workmen.'

'I am used, of course,' he said, 'to writing under conditions that would have stopped even Charles Dickens in his tracks.'

'I know, dear, and we're terribly proud of you,' replied his wife. 'But think what you might achieve during a period of total peace.'

'I cannot for the moment imagine what total peace is like,' said Mr Bagthorpe. 'But I think you are right. I must go, for everybody's sake.'

And so, to the amazement and ill-concealed

delight of the rest of the family, he wrote off accepting his prize and fixing a date a week hence for his stay. Once having decided to go, he was impervious to all quips and warnings from his unsympathetic family.

'Crikey, father, you've got a nerve,' William told him. 'They won't give you any food, you know. You'll come back half the man you are.'

'Or develop anorexia nervosa,' added Tess, 'which can be fatal, though admittedly more likely to be so in the case of an adolescent female, which you are not.'

'Debbie Beaumont's mother went to one of those,' chipped in Rosie. 'And Debbie says her eyes sunk all in.'

Grandma contented herself with being lofty. She was going to miss her son. He instigated a good seventy-five per cent of all Bagthorpian rows, and she needed someone to pit herself against.

'While not disputing that you have plenty of poisons in your system which require draining,' she said, 'I am disappointed, Henry, that you do not have the necessary will-power and Strength of Character to drain yourself. The Health Farm is the most expensive form of starvation known to man. You should stay at home and drain your own poisons, and send the hundreds of pounds saved to Oxfam.'

Mr Bagthorpe pointed out that the money involved was to be spent by Betta Orange Juice, not himself, and that he did not believe that Oxfam would be a cause that they would wish publicly to espouse.

'Let them send a thousand gallons of the Orange Juice to Oxfam, then,' replied Grandma, uncrushed. 'They could remove the labels, as you yourself did, Henry. Nobody can count on orange juice in this house any more.'

Mr Bagthorpe was adamant. He would go, he said, unless prevented by an Act of God (in the absence of Daisy). He would later regret this.

Other prizes began to arrive during the following week. Most of them were minor ones. There was, for instance, a spate of hairdryers at the beginning of the week, followed by a lot of leather diaries and three yoghurt-makers.

On Wednesday, however, Grandma and Daisy scored again, this time as purported regular users of a certain brand of toothpaste. This realized Mr Bagthorpe's own worst fears, particularly as the letter was promptly followed up by two men from

Generation Gap Fluoride Toothpaste. One was the PR man and the other a photographer. They wished to use photographs of Grandma and Daisy in their advertisements, and were going to be very disenchanted, as Mr Bagthorpe observed, when the Blue Lagoon Lanolin Enriched Toilet Soap people launched *their* new campaign.

'Somebody,' he said ominously, 'will probably sue somebody. Especially as you, mother, are wearing exactly the same dress and earrings as you wore for the Blue Lagoon photographs.'

Mr Bagthorpe was in a particularly bad mood that day after having failed to win a motorized caravan and ended up instead with a car tool kit.

'It will be as much use to me,' he said, 'as a pair of knitting needles to a penguin. A man of my temperament doesn't look under bonnets. All machines are infernal. Machines are the opium of the masses. If all the machines in England were thrown into the North Sea tomorrow, we should be back in the Garden of Eden. And the weather would probably improve.'

When William pointed out that it had been an illogical step for a man like Mr Bagthorpe to take on entering a Competition for any infernal machine, in the first place, he was ignored.

'I shall give that tool kit to Russell for Christmas,' Mr Bagthorpe said, cheering up a little at the thought. 'I'm running out of ideas for useless things to give him. He drives round the countryside doing ten miles to the gallon and maiming people left and right, and has never seen a carburettor, whatever that is, in his life. Let *him* get under his bonnet.'

He thus fulminated as Mrs Bagthorpe telephoned The Knoll to inform the Parkers of Daisy's latest triumph.

'She will be over in an hour,' she announced on her return. 'Celia wants time to tidy her up a little.'

'I should think so,' returned her husband. 'Are the child's teeth all her own?'

This was a gibe aimed at Grandma, who had naturally cheated in this Competition, this time to the extent of claiming all her teeth as her own. This was not true, as the whole family knew. Sometimes, in the kind of tense, drawn-out silence that cropped up so often in the household, Grandma would click her dentures around in her mouth to intensify things further.

'You told a deliberate falsehood,' said Mr Bagthorpe. 'False being the operative word.'

'Any woman would have done the same,'

175

returned Grandma calmly. 'It is our privilege. No one, I hope, will have the face to ask me to open wide?'

When Daisy arrived it was easy to see why Aunt Celia had required a whole hour for her adornment. Daisy had been got up, as Mr Bagthorpe observed, like a cross between Little Bo Peep and Goldilocks—the latter being an allusion to her hair, which had been prinked into tight ringlets and tied with two outstanding pink bows.

'Doesn't she look a lamb?' cried Grandma ecstatically.

'A wolf,' contradicted Mr Bagthorpe, 'in lamb's clothing.'

When the men from Generation Gap Fluoride Toothpaste arrived they were given coffee. As they drank it Mr Bagthorpe tried to bait them.

'In my opinion,' he told them, 'and I *am* a Man of Letters, the word "gap" in the name of your product would seem an unfortunate choice. I should not have thought that any manufacturer of toothpaste would have wanted the word "gap" in his advertisements.'

The two men exchanged uneasy glances which Mr Bagthorpe did not fail to note. He had made, he realized, a scoring point.

'No doubt,' he continued, 'the ill-considered use of this word has led to plummeting sales, and the drastic and desperate measure of trying to build up sales by the use of photographs of members of my family. Personally, I do not believe they will do anything for your sales.'

'Oh yes, sir, I'm sure they will,' said the PR man, with a gallant half-bow in the direction of Grandma, who was frigidly fixing her son. In the stony silence that followed Jack hoped fervently that she would not forget herself, and click her teeth.

The photographer had done nothing since he arrived but stare at Aunt Celia, who was looking particularly ravishing in full-length cheesecloth. In the end she must have become fidgety about this, and she left the room. At once the photographer began a whispered conversation with the PR man, who kept nodding his head. At last he looked at the Bagthorpes, who were already looking at him with undisguised interest, and said:

'Tim Scott Johnson, here, has had what I think is a perfectly valid and effective idea, and one we should perhaps adopt. In the original Competition, as you will remember, we asked only for entrants from two generations. If we were to have three, however, how much more effective our campaign would be.'

He again made a nervous bowing movement in the direction of a drawn-up Grandma.

'Would your daughter, perhaps, consent to taking part? On payment, of course, of a suitable fee.'

'Unfortunately,' replied Grandma, without batting an eyelid, 'dear Celia has lost half her teeth.'

Mrs Bagthorpe let out a little gasp at this slander and Grandpa, fortunately for his wife, did not hear it. Like most men, he tended to stick up for Aunt Celia.

'But they *look* natural enough,' insisted the photographer, clearly bent on having Aunt Celia in his lens.

'I should imagine,' Grandma turned to the PR man, 'that a certain moral issue is at stake here. Would you, may I ask, be happy to advertise your toothpaste with a smile that is, to your certain knowledge, false?'

She had him there. The session was completed without the presence of Aunt Celia, and Grandma smiled obligingly throughout, happy in the certainty that she ran no risk of being eclipsed by her own daughter.

'Besides,' she told the others later, by way of justification, 'they would certainly have made me look ten years older than I really am, if Celia had been there, to emphasize the gap. Any woman would have done the same.'

To which there was no answer—or none, at any rate, that Mr Bagthorpe could think of off the cuff.

The Toothpaste people must have been very pleased with the results of the photographic session, because they returned next day with a request that Grandma and Daisy should, for an extra fee of course, make a television commercial. This was not as flattering as it first appeared, because it transpired that the sole object was to get Aunt Celia's peerless features on to the screen and associated (one way or another) with Generation Gap Fluoride Toothpaste.

'If Mrs Parker,' pleaded the PR man, 'could possibly bring herself to appear, and say how much she regretted not having used Generation Gap and saved her teeth, it would be of immeasurable benefit.'

'I daresay,' replied Grandma, unmoved. 'But my daughter, naturally, has her pride. She is a presentable-looking young woman, and would not wish the world at large to know her secret. Daisy and I will make the commercial unaided.'

This, inevitably, was what happened. The PR man evidently considered the matter of Aunt Celia's false teeth too delicate a matter to broach to her personally, which was lucky for Grandma. The Bagthorpes all assembled to watch the making of the commercial, a project that involved an unconscionable number of people, from continuity girls to top-rank lighting cameramen.

'One would imagine,' remarked Mr Bagthorpe jealously, 'that one of my scripts was involved. Is nobody interested in *my* teeth?'

These were sufficiently bared during the process of filming to have attracted the attention of anyone who had been interested in them. The dialogue struck Mr Bagthorpe as particularly nauseating, and he offered to rewrite it.

'If I were to rewrite it,' he told the producer, 'and you gave me a credit, you would be reviewed in the Sundays. Everything I have ever written has been reviewed in the Sundays.'

The producer murmured feebly about Unions and Advertising Standards and apologetically ran Daisy and Grandma through their existing lines. These were footling to a degree, but the actresses involved clearly enjoyed saying them. One of the things Daisy had to say was, 'Oh, Grandma, what lovely *teeth* you've got!' which, as Mr Bagthorpe pointed out, sounded like something straight out of 'Red Riding Hood', and would arouse disappointed expectations in the viewer of Grandma's being metamorphosed into a wolf.

'She'd do that all right,' he told them.

The commercial took several hours to make, mainly because Daisy kept saying 'Grandma Bag' and the Toothpaste people did not want the 'Bag' in. Nor did the presence of Aunt Celia help. In the first place she distracted the film crew, and in the second she kept cooing and darting to adjust Daisy's ringlets after the clapperboard and 'Action!'

At the end of the session Grandma disappeared and came down a few minutes later wearing her fur coat.

'Off out, are you?' enquired Mr Bagthorpe. 'Going to get some fresh air to blow the sickening scent of commercialism from your nostrils?'

'I am going to tea with Daisy,' she replied. 'She has just invited me.'

Aunt Celia looked dubious at this. She had already formed the opinion, as had the Bagthorpes themselves, that Daisy and Grandma taken singly were to be reckoned with, but as The Unholy Alliance were not to be let out of sight. Matters had not been improved by the introduction of Arry Awk as Third Party. It seemed that his invisible presence would give the pair of them unlimited licence to do anything they wanted and then lay the blame on the defenceless Arry.

'Arry Awk,' Mr Bagthorpe declared, 'is an Archetypal Can-carrier. I should know. I'm one myself.'

'You may come to tea, mother,' said Aunt Celia, 'but I shall expect you to exert a proper influence. Poor little Daisy has been through a bad patch lately.'

At this Mr Bagthorpe let out one of his bitter laughs.

Grandma replied:

'Naturally, Celia. I am, after all, your mother, and think I know something about children. And Daisy and I are on the same wavelength. We understand one another perfectly. And I may as well tell you the main reason why I am coming to your house is that Daisy and I wish to write on walls, and we are not allowed to do it here.'

Mr Bagthorpe went into one of the longest speechless silences, as opposed to ordinary silences, he had ever been in.

Chapter 12

It was lucky for Mr Bagthorpe that he had left for Tallbuoys Health Farm just before the men came with the news about Zero. He himself believed, as he said later, that had he been present he would certainly have had a seizure or become demented.

'My hold on sanity is already fragile,' he said, 'and would have snapped.'

The rest of the Bagthorpes, who *were* present, were at first incredulous and then, inevitably, consumed with envy.

Rosie herself was delighted to begin with, especially as the men from Buried Bones dogfood had brought with them her prize. Mrs Bagthorpe was full of praise.

'Though I hope, Rosie,' she said, 'that you will not allow your interest in photography to take precedence over your Portraits. Your Portraits are truly creative and quite unique.'

'And anyone can take a photo,' added Tess.

It emerged, however, that the Buried Bones men

were interested not primarily in Rosie, but in her subject.

'Show us the dog,' they begged, once the congratulations were over. 'Is he real? Does he exist?'

'Fetch him, Jack,' said Mrs Bagthorpe resignedly.

Jack was pleased to escape. He had cringed when the Buried Bones men first fetched out huge blow-ups of Rosie's winning photographs. Tess and William had guffawed mercilessly, and the former shrieked:

'Wait till father sees them! Look at Uncle P holding up that biscuit—are you going to *publish* them? You're *not!*'

Jack went slowly upstairs, wondering how this was going to affect Zero's confidence. He could already feel it affecting his own.

It was a rotten thing to do to you, Zero old chap, he thought miserably. You'll be the laughing stock of England. And it's my fault, mainly.

Zero was guarding Jack's comics in his room. He had gone on guarding them long after the necessity to do so had expired. He seemed to have got it into his head that they were valuable, and Jack could not convince him otherwise. In any case, he thought, it was probably a good thing for Zero to *think* he had an important responsibility, even if he had not.

Jack sat on the edge of the bed and gave Zero a lot of patting and praising before he broke the news about the photographs.

'I didn't know Rosie was there, honestly,' he told him. 'It was a mean thing for her to do. But I'm in it as much as you are. We'll just have to stick together. Don't let it get your ears down.'

At last, reluctantly, he descended, Zero trailing behind.

Their reception was stunning. Instead of the derisory laughter and cutting personal remarks he had expected, Jack found that the Buried Bones men were almost beside themselves with enthusiasm.

'It's unbelievable!' yelled one.

'Get him outside—let me take some shots!' shouted the other.

A dazed Jack finally came to grasp that he had in Zero something that the world had been waiting for a long time.

'He's a gold mine, I tell you!' cried one.

'You're sure he's a mongrel?' enquired the other anxiously. 'He is unique?'

'He's that all right,' said William. 'Muttonbrained pudding-footed hound.' (He evidently felt entitled to use Mr Bagthorpe's lines in his absence.)

Nobody could quite take in what was happening, least of all Zero himself. He kept edging up to Jack, practically sitting on his feet and giving him little nervous licks.

Mrs Fosdyke, disgusted, told the men, 'You wouldn't believe the wiping up I do after that animal, feet that size!' but they were not sympathetic. They gave her to understand that before long the world would be queueing up for the privilege of wiping Zero's footprints up. What finally convinced the Bagthorpes of the seriousness of the Buried Bones' intentions was when one of them suddenly clapped a hand to his head and yelled:

'My God! Insurance! Is he insured?'

'Is he *what*?' said William. 'I doubt if he's even got a licence.'

'Quick, Bill,' urged the man with the camera. 'Get on to Head Office. Can we use the phone?'

The Bagthorpes listened unashamedly while Bill got on to Head Office and gave orders for Zero's immediate Insurance. What really created a silence was the sum he put on Zero's head. Zero, apparently, was worth one hundred thousand pounds.

Mrs Fosdyke, who was listening along with

everyone else, told her cronies later in the Fiddler's Arms, and it was evident from their reactions that they were not representative of the Great British Public confidently expected to become instant fanatical Zero Worshippers.

'Great ugly thing he is!' exclaimed Mrs Bates, 'and footmarks all over everywhere.'

'I should think they'll find their mistake soon enough,' predicted Mrs Pye sagely. 'Dogs in commercials is supposed to do what they're supposed to do, and that one never will.'

'I daresay,' said Mrs Fosdyke, unsoothed, 'but what about the taxpayers' money? A hundred thousand pounds! That's ten times my late hubby, and at least he was *human*!'

While Bill was discussing the finer points of the Insurance (ten thousand for loss of limb, fifty thousand for an eye, and so on) Grandma descended into the hall. Hearing large sums of money being thus bandied about, she leapt to the conclusion that somebody was making wills. As Bill was winding up the conversation she moved to the telephone and whisked it from him.

'Just one moment,' she said, 'I wish to alter *my* will. Are you there? Are you there?'

There followed much confusion. In the end

Grandma slammed down the phone, exclaiming, 'I shall not consult *that* solicitor again!' and went muttering into the kitchen in search of coffee.

'What are all these men doing here!' she asked, indicating the two Buried Bones. 'I must have my hair reset before there are any more photographs. Where is Daisy? What have we won this time?'

When she was eventually apprised of the situation she tried at first to capitalize on it.

'The situation is becoming ludicrous,' she said. 'Too many Competitions have been won. Daisy and I are becoming tired of the constant invasions of our privacy. We could, however, if you wished, offer your pet food to the dog. That way, the dog would not be too much in evidence. He is, after all, a mongrel.'

'He's worth a hundred thousand pounds,' Jack told her immediately, fortified by the knowledge that he at last now had something concrete to put forward in Zero's favour. 'He's just been insured for that.'

Grandma turned to Mrs Bagthorpe.

'How much am I insured for?' she demanded. 'Not that I could be replaced.'

Mrs Bagthorpe was saved from replying by the advent of the Happy Family people, whose visit was expected but had been forgotten in the general turmoil. They could hardly have arrived at a less auspicious moment, the only wholeheartedly happy people present being Jack and the Buried Bones men, and the latter did not count. Borderland Television was interested only in Happy Bagthorpes.

Fortunately the Buried Bones and the BTV pair got on very well to begin with, and there was much mutual congratulation between them on their fortunate discovery of the Bagthorpes. The whole family, in fact, overhearing themselves being discussed in this way, began to feel rather like newly upturned buried bones themselves. They began to wonder whether they had ever existed in their own right.

'They are exactly the kind of close-knit nuclear family we were hoping for,' enthused Sue.

'That dog,' said Buried Bones Man One solemnly, 'could only have been found in a family like this. We shall corner the market within weeks. Have you insured them?'

'Insured whom?' The Borderland Television pair looked blank.

When the Buried Bones explained, Sue and Jeremy immediately looked apprehensive. The seeds of doubt and fear had been sown.

'What if . . .' Buried Bones Two lowered his voice, '. . . something were to happen halfway through filming?' He lowered his voice further. 'There's been a spot of Fire and Flood about lately, if you look around. If people are accident prone, they're always having Fires and Floods. I think these people *are* accident prone.'

Grandma overheard most of this by dint of moving right in on the group.

'In my opinion,' she told Borderland Television, 'you should insure the entire family. I think a quarter of a million pounds would be a suitable sum.'

'Oh, mother!' exclaimed Mrs Bagthorpe. 'Don't be absurd!'

'It is a question of self-respect,' said Grandma obstinately, 'and a sense of dignity and worth. If I felt myself to be worthless, I doubt if I could bring myself to look happy and contented for any film.'

There followed a series of telephone calls to and from Borderland Television, and the Bagthorpe family were duly insured.

The week that followed was outstandingly awful despite the absence of Mr Bagthorpe. At times there were as many as forty people in the house, all ruthlessly pursuing their own business and all, quite frequently, at cross purposes. There were carpenters, plasterers, and decorators, all of whom wanted to get finished and have their bills paid before Christmas. There was a production team of twenty from Borderland Television who were themselves inexorably committed to producing a finished film for Christmas Day. And there was a team from Buried Bones who were hell bent on a commercial out in time for the big Christmas-viewing audiences. None of these people cared who got trodden down in the process, or whether the Bagthorpes themselves were left limp and drained, shadows of their former selves.

The man who turned up to direct 'The Happiest Family in England' was called PJ by the crew, and the Bagthorpes hated him on sight. The feeling appeared to be mutual. He had hardly been in the house half an hour before he lighted on the plain truth that the Bagthorpes were *not* the Happiest Family in England.

'Though you had better try and look it,' he told them. 'There is such a thing as breach of contract.'

By the end of the first day's filming the younger Bagthorpes were all for breaching the contract and taking the consequences, but their mother pleaded with them to go on, for all their sakes.

'If we make the effort, and act happy,' she said, 'we may well come to *be* happy. It is a known psychological fact. And besides, we want people to *think* we are happy, don't we? And besides, we *are* happy, really.'

Grandma was adamant that Daisy should figure in the film and the Parkers came over each day. This had a bad effect on Mrs Fosdyke who was now irremediably nervous in the vicinity of Daisy.

She was forced to act happy herself, on occasions. PJ decided that the Tin Shaking should be shown, as an example of the kind of zany, high-spirited larking the Bagthorpes went in for. On the day scheduled for the filming of this sequence Mrs Fosdyke arrived with her hair newly and drastically permed by Mrs Pye and prepared for the worst.

She went obediently through the routine of asking William, whose turn it was according to the Rota, to open a tin of apricots for dessert. The family, already seated at the table with spoons at the ready, waited for the inevitable minced beef or mushy peas to appear.

William, who considered that he had not so far figured sufficiently prominently in the film, made great play with the tin opener. He finally lifted the lid of the tin with something like reverence to reveal (his first-ever bull's eye)—apricots. The Bagthorpes, as one, broke into hysterical laughter and Mrs Fosdyke herself burst into tears. PJ fumed and swore and said it was a conspiracy and the whole sequence had to be filmed again, this time with Mrs Fosdyke sniffing and dabbing at her nose throughout.

It was this kind of thing that led to a kind of creeping madness in the Bagthorpe household. Each of its members, as the days went by, began to behave in an increasingly pronounced manner— to become, as it were, twice their usual selves. William, for instance, when not actually needed for filming, would go up to his room and beat out tattoos of hitherto unequalled frenzy and duration. Rosie took to doing unflattering but recognizable Portraits of PJ and leaving them scattered around everywhere, and Tess quoted from Voltaire in every third sentence and kept using words like 'incontrovertible' and 'charismatic'.

PJ tried to persuade Mrs Bagthorpe to get her husband back from the Health Farm, but this she steadfastly refused to do. She would not even divulge the name of the place where he was staying. This had been agreed before Mr Bagthorpe had left.

'I don't mind looking happy just once,' he said, 'if I can remember how. I'm used to sacrifices. I'll do my bit at the end.'

During the rest of the film Mr Bagthorpe was to appear only, as it were, by suggestion. The rest of the family, for instance, were made to tiptoe smilingly past his study door, with the implication that they recognized and understood that a creative writer was in there, creating. Even Mrs Fosdyke was made to do this, although her usual practice was to make as much rattling and banging as possible within earshot of the study as retaliation for the looks Mr Bagthorpe sometimes gave her.

PJ also did a close-up of the notice Mr Bagthorpe had pinned on the study door and read *LITTLE CHILDREN WHO COME UNTO ME SUFFER* as evidence of his delightful and whimsical humour.

Mrs Bagthorpe had rung her husband on his first evening and told him how well the Happy Family project was going. She did not, however, tell him about Zero.

There was no way, she thought, that any Health Farm would be able to help Mr Bagthorpe if he heard about Zero and the one hundred thousand pounds. She did not believe anybody would be able to help him.

On this occasion, he had begged her not to phone during the rest of his stay.

'Don't write, either,' he had said. 'I need silence. I need to feel my way back into being human again.'

Mrs Bagthorpe had thought this sounded hopeful, and was determined to co-operate. She resisted all attempts to invade his privacy, and looked forward to the end of the week when her husband would return to his family a changed man.

'Miracles,' she repeated to herself firmly and often, '*do happen!*'

Chapter 13

Zero's hour was now at hand. Jack exulted in the certainty. His dog was now, at last, to have his day.

His ears will never droop again, he thought. I shall let him watch the commercial every time it comes up. He can take a just pride in his own achievements just like everybody else.

Making the commercial (which turned out to be only the first of many) was an achievement anyone could have taken a just pride in. Rosie, taking photographs with her new equipment of the Buried Bones people trying to get Zero to act the way they wanted, realized that she could easily win a Competition with these pictures, too.

Jack was given an outline script to study, and asked to train Zero up to playing his part as much as he could. He had only two days to do this, because Buried Bones were in such a rush to launch their campaign.

The idea was that Jack and Zero were to be filmed walking along together in an idyllic setting, while an unseen voice said, 'Zero goes for a walk every day. He just loves it.' Then Zero, without Jack seeming to notice, was to stop suddenly, and sniff hard. He was then to start digging furiously, and turn up a packet of Buried Bones dog-biscuits. Jack, meanwhile, was to saunter off into the far distance oblivious of the fact that he was no longer accompanied, while the voice said, 'Zero likes walks, all right—but he likes Buried Bones better. Ask any dog.'

None of this was easy. The walking part was straightforward enough, but when Zero was supposed to stop dead in his tracks and sniff, complications set in. For one thing, Zero had been made nervous lately by the house being always full of noisy strangers, and stayed glued to Jack even more than usual. He did not want to stand there by himself sniffing while Jack walked off and left him alone with a lot of eccentric people with cameras. He did not even seem to want to sniff if Jack stayed with him. He just edged up and sat on Jack's feet and looked dolefully around.

'I don't think he's a very good actor,' Jack told the film people apologetically. 'I don't think he's going to be able to act sniffing.'

It was then suggested that a technique similar

to the one Jack had employed for training Zero to Fetch and Beg should be used. This entailed everyone present getting down on all fours and sniffing and snuffing around, while Jack urged 'Sniff, Zero! Good old boy, Sniff!'

Zero was completely thrown by this incomprehensible behaviour and went and hunched right up next to Jack and squeaked a little and kept wetting his lips.

The whole morning was spent like this. After lunch the director asked:

'Is there anything that really excites that dog? Does he ever get eager?'

'He does in the woods, sometimes,' Jack told him. 'He get eager when he sees squirrels.'

The unit trekked on foot, carrying all their equipment, to the woods. There, indeed, Zero did become excited. He seemed to forget what he was there for, and bounded off and started barking non-stop at the squirrels, as he always did. Jack was pleased.

'He *can* get excited, you see,' he told them.

'The only trouble is,' said the director wearily, 'that he's looking up in the air. I can't see any way he's going to turn up Buried Bones in the air.'

Someone had brought along two large mutton bones.

'If we can cover them up with soil, and get him sniffing after them, we'll be halfway there,' said the director.

Unfortunately this did not work. It was hard to tell *why* Zero did not want to sniff these bones out. He might just not have been very hungry, or he might have been over-excited by the squirrels. Whatever the reason, he did not sniff.

The film unit all sat down and had a think.

'We've got to think this thing through,' the director told them. 'We must have that dog. We could get a trained Alsatian to make this film in ten minutes flat. But we must have that dog.'

He sat a long time thoughtfully watching Zero as he made his futile lunges after squirrels running a full thirty feet above him.

'What we've been doing,' he finally announced, 'has been all wrong.'

No one contradicted what seemed a self-evident truth.

'I'm going to turn the whole idea upside down on its head.'

A respectful silence ensued.

'I am deliberately trying to keep my voice calm

and controlled,' he went on, 'because I have just come up with the most stupefying and sensational idea that I believe has ever been used in advertising. And I am dazed and shattered by the pure and immaculate simplicity of it.'

They all sat and waited. In the distance Zero barked on a high monotonous note.

'What would your reaction be,' went on the director, 'if I told you that we are going to film the truth?'

He held up a hand.

'No. Don't answer right away. Take your time. Think about it. Just take in the sheer enormity of the concept. We are going to make a true commercial.'

Jack took a quick look around. Everyone present was looking very concentrated and wise, and he made an effort to assume a similar expression himself.

'That dog,' went on the director discerningly, 'is not clever. He's a numskull. He's a great, clumsy, stupid, lovable numskull. You get the key word? *Lovable*. Now there is nothing lovable about being clever. Even if we did spend six months getting that dog to sniff and turn up Buried Bones, nobody would love him for it. He'd just be another ordinary, smart dog on a commercial. No. What we do, we ditch the whole script, and we capitalize on his assets.'

This is what happened. The Buried Bones people went away and came back the following day with not one but two film units. Then the second unit filmed the first one trying to get Zero to sniff. Everyone went down on their hands and knees again and sniffed and snuffed, and Zero just looked hopeless and was the only one *not* sniffing.

The director had written a new commentary. This time, the voice said:

'We wanted to show Zero digging up a packet of Buried Bones. But Zero is never going to play Hamlet. He can't act. We can't even get him to understand what we want him to do. Sniff! Come on, boy, sniff! You see? Hopeless. But there's one thing Zero doesn't have to act. He really *does* like Buried Bones. Here, Zero—good boy!'

At this point Zero never quite managed to capture the look of keen interest one might have expected. He had by this time had enough of filming, and it was beginning to show. He crunched the Buried Bones biscuit all right, but only in a resigned, world-weary kind of way. He definitely looked as if he were doing it for the fifth time in an hour.

To Jack's surprise, however, the director seemed enchanted by Zero's performance.

'My God!' he exclaimed after the final take. 'Just look at him!' (Meaning Zero.) 'I've never seen anything so understated in my life. He just threw the whole thing away. Olivier could take lessons from him when it comes to understatement. The whole thing is brilliant.'

He turned out to be right about this. After the first showing of the Buried Bones commercial the lines of Borderland TV were jammed all night with calls from people who wanted to give Zero a home. He had apparently given the impression of being orphaned and sad, and half England, it seemed, wanted to make him happy.

After the third or fourth showing the telephone enquiries were mainly about where one could get a dog exactly like Zero. Everywhere little children were sobbing themselves to sleep because they wanted one so badly, and their parents were trying to get hold of one for Christmas. They would pay anything, they said.

Breeders began to ring up, begging for details of Zero's parentage. They came and examined him and tried to work out the various strains that had come together to produce him. There was a fortune awaiting the man who could breed Zeros. No one seemed very hopeful about this.

'My guess,' said one of them gloomily, 'is that it's taken centuries of unbridled cross-breeding to produce that. This is the biggest single blow ever struck at the Kennel Club. It could even be mortal. No one wants our dogs any more.'

Buried Bones had posters made of Zero at his most bewildered-looking, and gave one away for every ten packets of their product bought. People with five children thus had to purchase fifty packets at one go, and the sight of people trundling through supermarkets with trolleys piled high with Buried Bones became a familiar one.

Owing to popular demand a Zero Fan Club was founded, called *Zero Worshippers*, and people got their photographs autographed with a large paw-mark, and badges saying 'I am a Zero Worshipper' or 'Absolute Zero' or 'Zero is the Most'.

None of this had any real effect on Zero. If anything, he became more dislocated than ever because of the habit people now had of suddenly diving at him in the street or in shops, and shouting, and causing crowds to form. These were friendly crowds, but could not have seemed so to him. Jack tried to fend them off by denying Zero's identity, but no one ever believed him. Sometimes Zero would be patted for half an hour on end. It was lucky, as Mr Bagthorpe pointed out, that whatever Zero's other shortcomings, he was not the sort that bit.

'If he was,' he said, 'then this country would be clean out of tetanus shots.'

His own attitude towards Zero did not change much. If anything, it was the same attitude as before, but now tinged with professional jealousy. Most weeks Zero commanded more viewing space than Mr Bagthorpe, and he was certainly better known. No crowds formed when Mr Bagthorpe went into town.

Grandma and Daisy got recognized, though, particularly when the former wore the outfit she had used for her Blue Lagoon and Generation Gap advertisements. Once she persuaded Daisy to wear her outfit as well, and the pair of them signed hundreds of autographs and a policeman had to come and control the crowd. Grandma talked about this a lot when she wanted to goad Mr Bagthorpe into a really first-class row.

'What a pity you are not photogenic, Henry,' she would say, or:

'To advertise toothpaste, one has to show one's

teeth, of course. People who never smile cannot expect much interest to be shown in them.'

At this Mr Bagthorpe would almost invariably bare his teeth.

'You and Daisy,' he would say, 'are novices. Within three months people will be sick of the sight of you. Have you not heard of over-exposure? Why do you think I curb myself as I do? I could have a script on every night of the week, if I wanted.'

'People will never get tired of Daisy and me,' Grandma replied. 'We are originals.'

(The man from Generation Gap had told her this, though at the time, of course, he did not know about the near-identical Blue Lagoon campaign.)

'Amen to that,' said Mr Bagthorpe grimly, and he left the room abruptly, because Grandma could cap anything—even the last word.

Chapter 14

Mr Bagthorpe did not, after all, have a whole ten days at the Health Farm feeling his way back into becoming human again.

The zealous Buried Bones, by way of advance publicity, managed to get going a news story about The Dog Insured for One Hundred Thousand Pounds. When Mr Bagthorpe opened his newspaper at orange-juice time and saw Zero gazing at him, he immediately shut his eyes, and kept them shut for a full two minutes. While his eyes were closed he thought frantically that he should have consulted his doctor before coming to the Health Farm.

'How do I know,' he wondered in anguish, 'whether I've got permanent brain damage? All that lettuce and carrot juice is not natural. Anyone creative should not tinker with his metabolism. Even if I open my eyes and find that hound isn't there, after all, I shall go home. I'm frightened.'

When he had taken in the fact that a large

photograph of Zero was indeed contemplating him mournfully from page four of his newspaper, he read the caption and, with mounting incredulity, the story.

He then told the Director of the Health Farm that he would have to return home immediately as there was a crisis in the family—which, if not strictly true, soon would be. When Mr Bagthorpe got home there was going to be a crisis.

He did not telephone his wife to warn her of his impending arrival. He wanted to catch everybody out at whatever they were up to the moment his back was turned and he himself weakened, probably permanently he felt, by a diet of nuts and water. This way he could also, of course, make a really effective entrance. He arrived home just as Grandma and Daisy were being Happy for the Borderland Television people. PJ had wanted them to be Happy separately, but Grandma refused.

'I can only be really Happy with Daisy,' she told him. 'And even then I will have to work myself up to being Happy first.'

'And how will you do that?' he enquired.

'There is only one way,' she replied.

This turned out to be a filmed lecture by herself in the form of a guided tour of the photographs of

Thomas in her room. There were dozens of these, all showing him at his worst—up a drainpipe baring his teeth, for instance, or practising unsheathing his claws, or staring malevolently into the lens or just looking plain Satanic. Grandma intended to wax exceedingly lyrical about him and if possible get him posthumously into a pet food advertisement, though she did not of course admit to this ulterior motive. PJ resisted the whole idea for as long as he could but in the end Grandma won.

'I am an old lady,' she said, 'and I think my wishes should be respected.' (She admitted to being old when it suited her, and then retracted later.)

PJ eventually gave in, consoling himself with the thought that Thomas would be a strong candidate for pride of place on the cutting-room floor, despite keen competition for this.

Once Grandma had warmed up to being Happy by dwelling on the life and times of the late Thomas, she came downstairs and allowed herself to be arranged for filming in the sitting-room with Daisy. The latter was given Rosie's china doll's tea-set and asked to pretend to have a tea party with Grandma. This looked like a good idea until Daisy started pouring cups of tea for Arry Awk.

"Ere you are, Arry,' she said, plonking down a cup and saucer in a space to her left. 'I've put you lots of sugar in I've put four lumps would you like five?'

'Daisy, dear,' said Grandma rather edgily, 'Arry Awk isn't *at* this party. There are just you and I, dear.'

'And Arry,' replied the incorrigible Daisy. 'He's a bad boy and jus' came without me asking.'

'I would like another lump of sugar, please,' said Grandma jealously. Daisy dropped one in and it splashed Grandma's frock but she did not remark on this.

'This is a delicious cup of tea, Daisy,' she went on, gamely sipping at her mixture.

'You're not really s'posed to drink it, Grandma Bag,' Daisy told her. 'It's all fings mixed up.'

Grandma uttered a little choking cry but kept her cool admirably, aware that the cameras were still turning.

'The chocolate biscuits are real, I think,' she observed. 'I would like one of those, please.'

'I don't fink there will be any left,' Daisy told her. 'They're Arry Awk's favourites.'

She thereupon crammed two in her own mouth and leaned over to put three on Arry Awk's plate and lost balance and knocked the teapot into Grandma's lap.

'Ooooh!' squealed Daisy. 'You *bad* boy, Arry Awk!'

'I think,' said Grandma dangerously, 'that Arry Awk had better go home. I think I may be getting near the end of my tether.'

'Cut!' shouted PJ. 'In the name of heaven, madam, can you not humour the child? It is the *child's* tea party, and you are supposed to be her indulgent grandmother being *Happy* with her.'

Grandma drew herself up.

'I contracted,' she told him distinctly, 'to look Happy with Daisy. There was no mention of a third party. I think I acted as Happy as anyone could reasonably have been expected to act, under the circumstances. It is not you who have to live with Arry Awk.'

'Am I to understand,' said Mr Bagthorpe, who had been watching the scene unnoticed, 'that Arry Awk is still with us?'

PJ turned and favoured him with a cool glance.

'Do you mind, sir?' he said. 'We are involved in a very difficult scene.'

'As long as you remain in this house,' Mr Bagthorpe told him, 'there is no way you are going to be able to avoid being involved in difficult scenes. This house, incidentally, being mine.'

'Henry never did have any sense of timing,' put in Grandma, hiding her delight at his reappearance.

'Aaaah!' Comprehension dawned on the face of PJ. 'Mr Happy Bagthorpe himself, I take it?'

'I am not happy,' returned Mr Bagthorpe curtly. 'Nor have I ever claimed to be.'

'But you said you wished you were, father,' Jack reminded him. 'You said you wished we could be happy like other families.'

'So I did,' agreed Mr Bagthorpe heavily.

Now that Mr Bagthorpe was home the chances of the family acting Happy for Borderland Television decreased hourly. Grandma *felt* Happy, but was careful not to show it. Grandpa was Happy too, but then he always was, which was why nobody ever took much notice of him. He went quietly on leading his own Happy life side by side with the rest of the family, running on a parallel track, as it were, with only occasional junctions. In the end there was quite a lot about Grandpa in the Christmas Day film because he was the only one (Daisy apart) who came over as genuinely Happy. All the others were overacting.

The hardest thing of all for PJ to achieve was

to get Mr Bagthorpe to do his little piece. Mr Bagthorpe, to do him justice, had originally intended to make an effort to co-operate. What had changed his mind was the subtle but definite alteration in his appearance that had been effected by his stay at Tallbuoys. Mr Bagthorpe had been lean and rangy to start with and had not needed to lose weight. It seemed, however, as the Director of the Health Farm had explained, that the process of draining poisons from anybody's system involved, necessarily, a loss of weight.

Mr Bagthorpe, then, was now hollow-eyed and interesting-looking as never before. He had not failed to remark this while shaving, and was on the whole pleased about it. He often wondered whether people took either himself or his work seriously enough. Now that he had a distinct touch of the consumptive about him, and was to appear on television, he thought that if perhaps he *acted* drawn and struggling with a daemon, his reputation would take a sharp upward turn.

Mr Bagthorpe and PJ therefore became locked in a deadly battle of wills, the former having the advantage because he was distinctly mettlesome after his period of fasting, and the latter approaching a state of stupefaction after a pounding week spent with Mr Bagthorpe's relatives.

When PJ, after a particularly haunted session in the study, shouted 'Hell, man, you're not the dying Keats!' Mr Bagthorpe was satisfied that he had struck the right note, and kept to it from then on. He tried acting in this pale and interesting way with his family as well, even when Borderland TV were not there, but cut no ice with them. In any case, he could only keep it up so long as he was not being goaded, and most of the time people were goading him.

Uncle Parker and Aunt Celia came round to collect Daisy after her abortive tea party. Mr Bagthorpe smiled wanly at them and tried to look short of breath.

'Good God!' exclaimed Uncle Parker.

'What is it, Russell?' asked Mr Bagthorpe faintly.

'You smiled! See that, Celia? There you are then— all they say about those places—it's all true! They've done a sterling job on you, Henry. Do it again.'

'Very funny.' Mr Bagthorpe was beginning to snarl already.

'They say,' mused Uncle Parker, 'that a strictly vegetarian diet lowers the aggressive impulse. Are you going to stick on it, now you've made a start?'

Mr Bagthorpe resisted rising to this, though a comment on the effects a vegetarian diet had had on Aunt Celia rose to his lips and was stifled only with difficulty.

Uncle Parker moved smoothly into top gear.

'And what about Zero, then, Henry?' he drawled. 'Made a bit of an error in our calculations there, didn't we?'

Mr Bagthorpe abandoned being the dying Keats and went into an unusually long and prosy piece about the values of modern society, ending up with the declaration that Zero would never, ever, add up to anything.

'You can quote me on that,' he said. 'You can have it in writing.'

His wife listened to this harangue with relief. She had been starting to worry about him, but realized now that he was his old self again.

'I'll make us all a nice cup of tea,' she said, as Borderland TV packed up for the day, 'and then we'll discuss our plans for Christmas. I think it would be nice if you and Celia, Russell, came to us for the day this year. Then we could all watch our programme together at teatime.'

PJ heard this. He paused by the door.

'Oh, by the way,' he said, 'we've got a new slant

215

we're going to use at the end. The boss thought it'd be a good idea if we came back here Christmas Day, and did the last five minutes of the show live.'

'I think that's a terrible idea,' said Mr Bagthorpe instantly. 'I don't like it.'

'I don't like it, either,' rejoined PJ. 'For one thing, I can think of ways I'd rather spend Christmas Day, and for another, I think it's courting disaster.'

'What is?' demanded Mr Bagthorpe aggressively. 'What d'you mean by that?'

'I mean,' returned PJ, 'that so far you have all acted Happy only when thoroughly rehearsed. May I ask you, as a matter of cold fact, whether you *do* contrive to be happy on Christmas Day?'

'Of course we do!' cried Mrs Bagthorpe.

'Certainly,' lied Mr Bagthorpe. He raised his voice to somewhere near a shout because William had just broken out on the drums overhead. 'You appear to have a very shallow view of happiness. You are mistaken, for instance, if you suppose the family not to be Happy at this present moment. People have different ways of being Happy.'

Mrs Bagthorpe was so touched by this speech that she edged up to him and squeezed his hand, which he instantly snatched away.

'Happy, are you?' said PJ cuttingly.

'You try proving we're not,' replied Mr Bagthorpe calmly.

'Dealt with him all right, Henry,' said Uncle Parker handsomely when PJ had gone. 'Check and mate, I thought.'

'You were marvellous, father,' agreed Tess. 'That man is malevolent, excruciating, and non-essential to the nth degree.'

The Bagthorpes were thus temporarily united against a common enemy, which was better than not being united at all. And when Mrs Fosdyke entered to announce that there were only two remaining unlabelled tins in the pantry, the gloom lightened further.

'Just think,' sighed Rosie, 'at Christmas we'll be able to *choose* what we eat. We'll be able to have real mince pies.'

'If you'll just come and give 'em a shake, then,' said Mrs Fosdyke to Tess, whose turn it was, 'you can have your teas.'

'There's no *need* to shake them,' Tess pointed out. 'They're going to be opened anyway, aren't they?'

Mrs Fosdyke had not thought of this. She looked baffled for a minute, then nodded, and scuttled off back to the kitchen. The two tins turned out to be both cling peaches, which was not a bad way to end the Tin Shaking era, and everyone was sitting round in pleasurable anticipation when the front door knocker banged.

'Would you believe!' exclaimed Mrs Fosdyke. Like Mr Bagthorpe, she thought people who visited the house did it only to annoy. Everyone got on with the meal while she went off to deal with the intruder. A minute or two later she was back.

'I've let 'im in,' she announced. ''E's in the 'all.'

'Who is it, Mrs Fosdyke?' enquired Mrs Bagthorpe, rising.

'It's a Mr Sugden,' she replied, 'and I think he's for you. 'E said something about a problem, anyhow.'

'But I only deal with Problems by post!' Mrs Bagthorpe none the less patted her hair and went out. She was gone quite a long time, in fact so long that she was forgotten and all the cling peaches were eaten up. When she returned Zero was just Begging for the last morsels of jam roll. Uncharacteristically, her eyes went straight to him.

'Oh dear!' she murmured. 'Oh *dear*!'

'What is it, mother?' asked Jack, who could see nothing wrong with Zero's performance.

'Oh, Jack, dear, I hardly know how to tell you. It's dreadful!'

'Have a cup of tea,' suggested Mr Bagthorpe, not without a degree of sarcasm.

'Is it something to do with Zero? Who is it?' asked Jack.

Mrs Bagthorpe sat down suddenly.

'I think you had better go and talk to him,' she told her husband, 'and see what you make of him. Oh, what a thing to happen, after all this time!'

'I don't know anybody called Sugden,' said Mr Bagthorpe. 'Why should I go and talk to him? Who, Laura, *is* Mr Sugden?'

She avoided Jack's eye.

'He says . . . he says—that he's Zero's real owner! And he says he wants him back!'

At this there was a really long silence. The Bagthorpes, for once, were lost for words. They were also, to their own astonishment, finding themselves in the grip of deep and conflicting emotions—with the exception of Jack himself, whose feelings were perfectly straightforward. He loved Zero, had always loved him, and that was that. The rest of the family, however, genuinely despised Zero and had no feelings of affection for him whatsoever—or so they had thought until the news that he might suddenly be taken from them for ever forced their real feelings to the surface. These feelings took them by surprise. Rosie was the first to speak.

'He's not—he can't be—he's *ours*!' she cried, and promptly burst into tears.

'The man's raving,' said Mr Bagthorpe tersely. 'Show him out, Mrs Fosdyke.'

She did not move. She knew, as did everyone else there present, that the man in the sitting-room possibly *was* Zero's real owner. Zero had simply appeared one day two years previously in the Bagthorpes' garden, and stayed. They had advertised him in the Lost and Found column of the local paper, but nobody seemed to have recognized the description, or come forward if they had. At the time, Mr Bagthorpe had thought this understandable.

'If ever *we* get a chance to lose him,' he had said, 'we'll take good care *we* don't get him back through any Lost and Found column.'

'Whatever shall we do?' This Problem was beyond Mrs Bagthorpe.

'He's not having Zero,' Jack said. 'I'd die first. I'm going to go and tell him so.'

He felt all at once very brave.

220

'Come on, Zero.'

Jack went out and Zero trailed after him. The others followed.

A short, balding man with a waistcoat button missing was planted on the hearthrug with his back to the fire. As Jack entered, he caught sight of Zero and exclaimed loudly:

'Cuddles! Cuddles, old boy—it's you!'

'It's *what*?' Jack was incredulous.

'*Cuddles?*' repeated Mr Bagthorpe disgustedly. 'You're mad.'

Mr Sugden ignored them. He concentrated on Zero, who was still at Jack's side and had remained totally untouched by his effusive greetings.

'Hey! Cuddles—come on, old chap—it's me. Come on. Walkies, boy, walkies.'

'It is no use your using trigger words in the hope that the animal will wag his tail and appear to recognize you,' Mr Bagthorpe told him coldly. 'That dog responds to no trigger words known to man. If you had been his true owner, you would have known that.'

Mr Sugden now turned his attention from the apathetic Zero and looked at Mr Bagthorpe instead.

'You aren't casting aspersions, I hope,' he said belligerently, 'on my rightful ownership?'

'That's right,' agreed Mr Bagthorpe. 'I am.'

'He doesn't know you,' put in Jack. 'You can tell he doesn't.'

'Not to be expected, after all this time,' countered the visitor. 'He'll soon come round, won't you, Cuddles, old chap?'

'Stop *calling* him that, will you?' snapped Mr Bagthorpe.

At this point Grandma stepped in.

'I can read you, sir,' she addressed herself to Mr Sugden, 'like an open book, I fear.'

'Oh yes, madam?' he returned, aggressively enough; though with a slightly hunted air, confronted as he now was by the entire Bagthorpe ménage in a solid phalanx.

'You have read,' Grandma told him, 'of the animal's unprecedented rise to fame. You have read the accounts—grossly exaggerated, I might say—of the large sums of money he earns. You have also read that he appeared in our garden as a stray. I think we can all put two and two together.'

'You are quite mistaken,' replied Mr Sugden. 'I recognized his picture, certainly. He hasn't changed a whisker. My wife broke down and cried when she saw him on the telly.'

'If you are claiming ownership,' put in Tess

surprisingly, 'presumably you will not object to establishing that ownership by answering a few pertinent questions. Perhaps, for instance, you can tell us what is his favourite food?'

'Well. Yes.' Mr Sugden appeared slightly shaken. 'It's been a long while, of course—difficult to remember—but yes, I think I can. Liver.'

'A fair guess,' said Mr Bagthorpe.

'Wrong!' crowed Mrs Fosdyke triumphantly. 'Garlic sausage!'

'He never had that at our house,' blustered Mr Sugden. 'We never go in for foreign stuff.'

'That dog'd eat toadstools if they'd a sprinkle of garlic on 'em,' continued Mrs Fosdyke, pressing her advantage with the ruthlessness of a seasoned prosecution counsel, 'and he must've got the taste for it *somewhere*.'

'Can he, for instance,' interposed William smoothly, 'fetch sticks when they are thrown?'

'Of course he can.' Mr Sugden immediately regained confidence. 'All dogs can fetch sticks.'

'Good morning, Mr Sugden,' said Mr Bagthorpe with an air of finality. 'Mrs Fosdyke will see you out.'

'Now just a minute!' Mr Sugden was advancing now, fumbling in his jacket pocket. 'Take a look at this! What about this, then?'

He was waving a photograph. Mr Bagthorpe stepped forward and snatched it, and the rest crowded round. It showed a modern bungalow, Mr Sugden and a woman who was presumably his wife, and sitting in the foreground doleful and unmistakable, Zero himself.

'Well?' It was Mr Sugden's turn to sound triumphant. The others were still staring disbelievingly at the photograph and trying to find some point of dissimilarity between the dog in the foreground and Zero himself.

Jack could not believe his eyes. He knew quite certainly and instinctively that Zero had never lived with this man and been called Cuddles and fetched sticks. Yet there he was. Jack was bewildered and at the same time suddenly chilled. The photograph looked like proof. Anyone who did not know Zero as Jack did would surely say that it *was* proof.

'Well?' Mr Sugden had his thumbs in his waistcoat now and it was easy to see how he lost buttons.

'Give it me,' came Rosie's voice.

She took the photograph and held it away from her, then near, half squinting her eyes with a professional air.

'It's a fake,' she finally announced. 'It's trick

photography. Someone has used one of the publicity photos of Zero and superimposed it on another negative.'

'Now look here!' Mr Sugden made to snatch the photograph away but Rosie deftly swooped it out of reach.

'It's easy, actually,' she continued with the utmost self-possession. 'I could do it myself.'

'Oh, Rosie!' Jack wanted to hug her but knew she would not thank him.

'If this is going to be your attitude,' blustered the visitor, 'I'm not at all sure I want the dog.'

'Good,' said Mr Bagthorpe. 'And I'm not sure that I'm not going to prefer charges for fraudulent impersonation. Hadn't you better leave before I come to a decision?'

Mr Sugden, who was now interestingly red in the face, moved quickly and reached the front door even before Mrs Fosdyke, though she was there in time to give it a thoroughly satisfying slam behind him.

'Rosie, darling, how clever of you!' exclaimed Mrs Bagthorpe. 'Fancy your detecting that the photograph was a fake!'

'I didn't,' she replied simply. 'I guessed. But I was right, wasn't I?'

'That hound—' Mr Bagthorpe was eyeing Zero with all his old weariness—'has been nothing but trouble since the day he came. Why in the name of heaven didn't we let him go while we had the chance? Must've been a brainstorm.'

Jack, bending to pat Zero to hide his emotion, heard this, but did not believe it. He could never again quite believe the things his family said about Zero. It seemed to him that this day had been the most triumphant of Zero's life—more of a landmark, even, than the day he was discovered by Buried Bones.

'They stood by you in your hour of need,' he told Zero exultantly in the privacy of his room. 'Every one of them—even Grandma, even William. They would have fought for you to the death. Just you remember that, old chap.'

He was going to have to, of course. The Bagthorpes, Zero's future secured, reverted at once to their former stances, and Mr Bagthorpe would often, in years to come, refer bitterly to the day when he had the chance of ridding himself of Zero, and passed it by. On one of these occasions Jack reminded him that he had fought as hard as anyone to keep Zero, but he denied it.

'I was simply testing the fellow out,' he

maintained. 'That might be the most mutton-headed non-productive hound that ever went on four legs, but it was the least I could in all conscience do. I am a humane man, I hope, and a fair one.'

Jack did not reply to this but was, for once, actually inclined to believe that it might be true.

Chapter 15

The Season of Goodwill was now relentlessly approaching and the Bagthorpes were labouring under an even stronger than usual sense of impending doom. They seemed hedged about left and right by deadlines. On top of all the last-minute Christmas preparations they had to contend with a battalion of workmen in the house, a continual spate of unwanted prizes, and above all the certainty that when Christmas Day did finally come, all would not be joy unconfined. PJ and Borderland Television would presumably see to that.

The buying of gifts had been to some extent simplified this year by the presence in the house of the prizes so far won and surplus to the Bagthorpes' own requirements. They were stacked in the dining-room and it looked, as Mr Bagthorpe observed, as if somebody were getting married and had forgotten to send out a Wedding Gift List.

'Who, for instance,' he enquired, 'has had the

lack of foresight to send off ten entries for toast-racks in a household where the general gluttony is such that no toast ever gets as *far* as a rack? No one in this house who depended on toast getting as far as a rack could ever survive.'

'They were runners-up,' Tess told him. 'They could have been a dishwasher. We can give them as presents.'

They did, though not to one another. A good deal of ingenuity went into the sifting of the winnings and matching of each to a suitable recipient. All three yoghurt-makers, for instance, went to Aunt Celia, with the words FIRST RESSERVE and SECOND RESSERVE carefully painted on two of them by Rosie.

'She'll think it's a proper set of three,' she told the others with satisfaction. When it was pointed out that the professionalism of the job was somewhat dissipated by the unorthodoxy of the spelling, she replied:

'It's Olde Worlde. Aunt Celia will like it. She likes poetry.'

Mr Bagthorpe's tool kit was, as he had promised, designated for Uncle Parker, though Jack himself secretly bought him a floral cravat to match his lavender suit. As parcels arrived, from now on people took them to some hidden corner before unwrapping them, in case there was a usable Christmas gift inside. No one was very much looking forward to opening presents this year. They were all well aware that as they were doing, so they would be done by.

The renovation of the house proceeded relatively smoothly up until December 17th, when Mr and Mrs Bagthorpe were rash enough to go into Aysham with their children, leaving Daisy alone with Grandma and Grandpa. Both the latter soon fell asleep and Daisy inevitably, once she had finished mixing Mrs Bagthorpe's face powder into the flour bin because it smelt as if it would taste nice, set off in search of a real challenge in the way of Reconciling the Disparate.

The decorators were finishing a room upstairs and Daisy first went up and enquired whether she might help. This offer they declined with spirit. They were by now aware that it was Daisy's handiwork they were currently attempting to remove all trace of, and were at last within sight of this goal. They were not, however, aware of just how deadly Daisy could be at her most creative, and illadvisedly told her to go and paint something of her own.

Daisy did not, of course, have her own paints with her, but she trotted off to Rosie's room to see if there were any oil tubes lying loose there. Disappointed to find only one tube of purple, from which she could squeeze only sufficient to daub a flower on the door with her finger, she went back downstairs.

All the decorators' materials were scattered untidily on a large dust-sheet in the still uncarpeted dining-room. Each tin of paint (the colours of which had been lovingly blended by Mrs Bagthorpe herself) had been carefully labelled to avoid confusion: SITTING ROOM WINDOW WALL, MASTER BEDROOM WALLS 1 & 2, and so on. The hall was already finished, but there was still a couple of inches of terracotta paint left in the tin. This Daisy carefully transferred to a large, almost full tin labelled DINING ROOM ALL FOUR WALLS. Using one of the rods she stirred it thoroughly in, and was eventually rewarded by seeing the colour transformed to a murky khaki.

She later said that this was meant to be 'toad colour' and that it had been Arry Awk's idea.

'He thought you'd like it,' she said. 'He likes toads best of anything and he's being a good boy like Mummy said or he won't get anything in his Christmas stocking.'

When Mr Bagthorpe learned that Arry Awk intended to hang up a stocking, he swore that he would personally ensure that it was filled to the brim with toads, and probably would have done, had the thing been feasible.

Daisy had only just finished Reconciling the Disparate tins of paint when the decorators came down to put the final coat on the dining-room.

'Rum shade,' said one of them, dubiously eyeing the toad colour.

'There's more than shades rum around this place,' returned one of his mates. 'Rummiest lot I've ever come across, that's definite.'

No one could dispute this, and so the four of them divided the toad colour into their individual tins and set about the transformation of the dining-room.

The Bagthorpes arrived home late in a cheerful mood with Christmas trees on the roof rack and a carrier full of food from the Chinese take-away. The decorators had by then finished for the day, and Grandma and Grandpa were watching television while Daisy wrote her latest thoughts on the back of Christmas cards.

Mrs Bagthorpe immediately tripped into the dining-room to inspect the progress of work, and almost swooned on the spot. With the bare floor, unshaded lights and toad walls it looked, as Mr Bagthorpe said, a veritable hell hole.

'There is no question of my ever eating anything in there,' he told Mrs Bagthorpe. 'I could not down a single mouthful within walls of that shade. Have you gone mad, Laura?'

Mrs Bagthorpe, who prided herself on her taste in general and colour sense in particular, was so maddened by this that she and her husband were soon well into an all-out row, while the strains of 'Silent Night, Holy Night' floated out from the television next door and the Chinese food congealed in its carrier. Just as Daisy's guilt was finally established Uncle Parker and Aunt Celia arrived to collect her, and all hell broke loose.

The row ended with Aunt Celia (who now immovably maintained that she believed in Arry Awk—and for that matter, probably did) bearing Daisy off in her arms and screaming over her shoulder at Mr Bagthorpe:

'You are a destroyer of innocence! You are a worm within the bud!'

Mr Bagthorpe followed the retreating Parkers to the front door and yelled after them:

'And don't you come back till Christmas Day,

I warn you! If I see you back here again before Christmas Day, I'll—'

The last part of the message of goodwill was mercifully drowned by the roar of Uncle Parker's exhaust and the spinning of tyres on violently scattered gravel.

The Parkers did not return until Christmas Day and when they did Mr Bagthorpe was placed in the mortifying position of presenting to Uncle Parker a tool kit that was not wanted in return for a case of extremely expensive vintage port that clearly was. There are few more untenable positions than that of receiving a costly and desirable gift from an adversary. Mr Bagthorpe's expression on opening up his gift was, being a mixture of gratification and a reluctance to appear gratified, a unique grimace. Uncle Parker, on the other hand, affected extreme delight at his own offering.

'By Jove!' he exclaimed. 'Really, Henry, old chap, you shouldn't have. Just the sort of thing one always *wants*, don't you know, but never quite likes to treat oneself to.'

Which, while being true of the case of vintage port, was certainly not true of the tool kit, as Mr

Bagthorpe well knew, and Uncle Parker knew he knew, and Mr Bagthorpe knew Uncle Parker knew he knew.

The atmosphere, then, was highly charged even before Christmas dinner began. None of the Bagthorpes had been particularly taken with their gifts, with the exception of those given by the Parkers, which had been intentionally chosen for their costliness and covetability, and had nothing to do with Competition Entering. Every one of them had a giant suntan oil from William (who was no longer getting answers to his letters to Atlanta) even including Grandma and Grandpa, though the latter at least had the grace to look pleased by this offering.

Matters were not improved by the fact that Christmas dinner was to be partaken of in the kitchen while the dining-room was being dressed for Christmas tea by a sulky and hungover crew from Borderland Television. Mrs Fosdyke had herself laid out the table on the previous day with all the best silver and china in the hopes of impressing Mesdames Pye and Bates who would undoubtedly be watching the programme at five o'clock.

'Though what it'll all look like,' she lamented, 'with walls the colour of stewed liver, I don't know.

If that Daisy was drowned at birth it'd be no more than she deserves.'

She was clearly regretful that the moment for this operation to be carried out had already passed.

The Borderland TV people props department were adding details of their own, including candles, Mrs Fosdyke noted with trepidation, and crackers.

'You watch out!' she hissed into the ear of a mystified Borderland man. 'There's a pyrotechnic in the house!'

She was alone in her misgivings, however, because the Bagthorpes had made the fatal mistake of thinking that Daisy had shot her final bolt for the current calendar year in perpetrating the toad walls. Daisy herself was very carefree and happy. She brought most of her presents and those of Arry Awk along with her, laid them out on the sitting-room floor and was Reconciling them, with the willing aid of Grandma. All she had time to do before dinner was tip three jigsaws out and mix all their pieces together, and this assured the others that the procedure would keep Daisy quiet for longer than if she solved the three puzzles separately.

Mrs Bagthorpe always took Christmas very seriously and had three trees in the house, all real, one each in the sitting- and dining-room and one in the hall.

'I love the house to smell of real fir!' she would sigh ecstatically. 'Such nostalgia!'

Usually the trees were lit with fairy lights, but this year she had insisted on old-fashioned candles for the dining-room, where the Bagthorpes were to be shown to the Nation being overwhelmingly Happy over the Christmas Tea.

'There are little children all over England who have never seen candles flickering on a Christmas tree,' she said, 'and never known their magic. Think, Henry, think, Mr Jones (PJ's real name, which, for obvious reasons, he did not use in such a competitive milieu), it may bring about a revival!'

Whether or not it did was never established, but it certainly brought about other consequences that could in no way be described as a revival. It had been arranged that this year each member of the family should receive an extra gift, from Borderland TV (up to the value of £10 per head), and that these should be placed about the candlelit tree. After a minute or so's live film of the Bagthorpes being Happy round the Christmas cake and mince pies, these presents were to be opened. No one but the props man knew what was in these enticing-looking boxes, though they had been shaken around a lot during the few days they had been in the house. Each member of the family, however, had privately told the props man what he or she would most like to receive, and there was no real reason to suppose that these wishes had not, in general, been granted. The Bagthorpes, indeed, were looking forward to opening these parcels.

At one o'clock, when Mrs Fosdyke was due to dish up the dinner, most adults present were considerably elevated by the liberal dispensation of spirits. Mrs Bagthorpe herself, being more than usually nervous and determined that things should go with a Dickensian swing, handed out more than usually plentiful potations of home-made punch, and she was not, of course, to know that Borderland TV had brought their own supply of stuff in anticipation of a hard and depressing day. Mr Bagthorpe felt himself both bound and inclined to open one of his bottles of vintage port after the well-brandied Christmas pudding. The result of all this was that the adults spent most of the afternoon sleeping— even Aunt Celia who had evidently been affected by auto-suggestion after drinking a bottle of her own elderflower champagne.

Teatime, then, was soon upon the Bagthorpes,

and found them still sleepy and not fully on their guard. At four o'clock the make-up girl started work on Grandma, who had expressed a wish to appear looking as much as possible like Dame Sybil Thorndike, followed by Mr Bagthorpe who asked her, *sotto voce*, to emphasize the already considerable hollows under his eyes. By 16.55 hours the entire gathering was seated round the festive board (Grandma and Daisy both wearing their Blue Lagoon and Generation Gap outfits in the certainty of being recognized and receiving fan mail). It was very hot and cramped in there, what with the lights, camera, and production team, and the jellies and icings were already beginning to melt. From 17.00 hours to 17.25 the family were to eat their tea in the usual way, while watching their filmed performances on one of the three monitor sets that were placed about the room.

When the credits began to roll on to the screen with first of all the title HAPPY CHRISTMAS HAPPY BAGTHORPES followed by a list of the names of everyone present, Mrs Fosdyke, who had had her tots along with everyone else but did not really have the head for it, began to sniff loudly.

'You'd better cut that out before 17.25,' PJ warned her in a savage whisper, and took a long consolatory swig at his beer. (All the crew were drinking beer now because they said the strong lights dehydrated them.)

The family chewed steadily, their eyes fixed on the screen. They were quite pleased with what they saw but not so pleased with what they were eating. Mrs Bagthorpe's face powder had definitely affected the flavour of the pastry and this was particularly noticeable in the case of the sausage rolls. They all reached first for one of these (with the exception of Grandpa, who started straight in on the stuffed eggs) and were naturally made unhappy when they found them all but inedible. When Mrs Fosdyke noticed that no one was finishing them, and that dark looks were being directed towards herself, *she* became unhappy too, and started sniffing again.

By 17.20 hours each of them had a hand on a cracker as if on a trigger. When the studio announcer said 'and now, over to the Happy Bagthorpes, live at home . . .' they were all to pull them and appear extremely jolly and put on their paper hats. Mr Bagthorpe, noting with satisfaction that his dying Keats performance was coming over well, mentally resolved not to do this.

'Keats could never, ever, have worn a paper hat,' he decided.

Jack had been requested by his mother to hold Zero's collar while the crackers were being pulled.

'We don't wish a repetition of Grandma's Birthday Party,' she had said smilingly. 'Not that history ever repeats itself.'

As PJ started the countdown to 17.25 hours the atmosphere became electric. The production assistants moved in and lit the Christmas tree candles, though they looked less than magical under the harsh glare of lights.

At a warning signal from PJ crackers were raised and as he dropped his arm as if holding a starter's flag, the Bagthorpes went into action. Crackers were pulled if not with hilarity at least with a lot of shouting and confusion that could easily pass as hilarity. Grandma pulled so hard that her arm ended up in a half-melted jelly and Aunt Celia jibbed at pulling her cracker and put both hands over her ears instead. Jack, with one eye on a monitor, noted that a bottle of beer inadvertently left on the table by the sound man was figuring largely in the foreground of the shot, and releasing Zero's collar, stretched out to remove it. He knew his mother would not want the nation to see beer bottles on her tea-table.

What happened next was never really very clear

afterwards, but it had something to do with Zero understandably backing away from all the banging and shouting and getting his paws inextricably wound in the flex leading to the boom. The man holding the boom did not notice this, but, finding himself short of flex, gave the boom a jerk to release it, and in so doing caught the top of the candlelit Christmas tree. From then on, history did not so much repeat as excel itself.

PJ alleged afterwards during the Insurance investigation that if the Bagthorpes had kept their heads none of the things that did happen would have happened. Nobody at the time seemed to be keeping their heads. Everybody screamed and shouted and fought to get clear of the blazing tree. Mr Bagthorpe hurled his tea at it and the production team threw their beer but not before the glittering and highly inflammable wrappings on the Borderland parcels had caught fire.

'Dial 999!' yelled Mr Bagthorpe and gave the table cloth a mighty yank so that food and crockery flew out at everybody. At the time, the rest thought he had yanked the cloth off because he had become unhinged, but what he had intended, apparently, was to throw it over the flames and stifle them. But before he could wrench it away from William and Uncle Parker, who were both hanging grimly on to it in case he did something rash with it, Daisy's fireworks had started to go off. There was nearly twenty pounds' worth of these because Daisy had persuaded Borderland TV to give them to Arry Awk as well as herself.

Up to this point everyone had acted as if the situation could eventually be salvaged and the cameraman in fact kept on filming the whole time. Even after the fireworks started going off and the dining-room had hastily been evacuated he stood in the doorway filming and a lot of what he shot was used later, on the News. (The Bagthorpes' tea party had now definitely crossed the frontier between Light Entertainment and News, and Jack could see from the one remaining monitor that their transmission had been cut, and an orchestra was playing instead.)

When the firemen arrived three of them turned out to be those who had come to put out Grandma's Birthday Fire, and when they saw all the rockets going off and blue and green lights glowing and so forth, you could see that they were so bewildered they could hardly do their job properly. Nearly all the ingredients of this fire were identical to those of Grandma's; only details differed, like its being Mr Bagthorpe rather than Zero who dragged the tablecloth off.

When the fire was out the firemen would not stay even for a drink. They said this was because they were on duty, but it was obvious that the real reason was that the Bagthorpes made them nervous. The Borderland people packed their blackened equipment in a daze and stumbled off into the night. Before he left, PJ told the Bagthorpes that they had probably ruined his whole life.

'No man should ever have his worst fears realized,' he told them, 'and that is what happened to me today. From now on, I shall be a cynic. All my natural optimism has vanished at a stroke. You have destroyed my faith in life.'

None of the family felt particularly repentant about this, but Mrs Fosdyke's equally shattered faith was something that struck much nearer home.

She had shrieked out her notice several times during the course of the fire, but the distractions were such that no one had paid any attention. At some stage she must have packed her bag and silently crept away, because when the Bagthorpes were left confronting the all too familiar sodden ruins of the dining-room she was suddenly registered as missing. Mrs Bagthorpe wanted her husband to take the car and go after her, but he refused.

'I'm in shock,' he told her. 'I am in no fit condition to drive a car.'

He persisted in this refusal and in the end Mrs Bagthorpe decided that as Mrs Fosdyke must almost certainly be in shock too, it might be better to wait a while before making any overtures.

'Though my Christmas will be quite spoilt by the uncertainty,' she said. 'I cannot possibly continue with my Problems without the assistance of Mrs Fosdyke.'

And so Christmas Day drew to a close with the door of the burnt-out dining-room finally closed and everybody in the sitting-room allotting blame for the events of the day and arguing endlessly. The television was switched on for the News, and there they saw the whole awful scene re-enacted and all started pointing and yelling 'Look—there you are—see that?' and so on. William announced his intention of asking the Borderland people to do an Action Replay at a private showing.

The News finished and a commercial came on. The battered Bagthorpes stared numbly at the close-up of Zero gazing at them from the screen. Unhurriedly *he* scrunched his Buried Bones.

'By Jove!' exclaimed Uncle Parker. 'Keeps *his* cool. Shows the lot of us up.'

'I do not accept that,' Mr Bagthorpe told him. 'The hound is an idiot, and it shows. And seeing him on the screen is all I needed to round off my day. I shall go to bed, so that the New Year will come more quickly. I have never before so strongly needed to make a fresh start with a clean slate. I consider my present state to be as near rock-bottom as it has ever been.'

Later, the family discovered that he had written on the wall in the hall on his way up to bed. (There was to be a fresh spate of writing thoughts on walls as a natural outcome of the fire.)

What he had written, was:

Hell is absolute zero.

The others could sympathize with this sentiment, but Grandma, when nobody was looking, penned sanctimoniously underneath:

No, Henry, hell is oneself

under which during the course of Boxing Day Mr Bagthorpe unguardedly wrote:

That depends who you are of course

beneath which, inevitably, Grandma wrote:

Precisely, Henry

and drew under it a thick, triumphant line punc-
tuated with a daisy, like a full stop.